Benzer an ... .

"When ... r the third time.

"Any minute, I hope!" We were as eager as Franklin to get started on his American Heritage badge, and we'd made plans to go to the new Grey County Museum. I pulled my notebook out of my back pocket and reread the list I'd written last night. It was short.

The Verified Truth about the Mayhews

1. Ancestors of steel, according to Mrs. Hall.
2. Family has lived in the same house for 175 years.
3. Relatives sold off most everything at an auction.
4. WM may have been a thief.
5. WM wrote a letter to Louise telling her to be careful. (Maybe <u>she</u> was a thief too?)
6. The house will be demolished unless I figure out a way to stop it.

I stuffed it back in my jeans. Hopefully, we'd learn more at the museum.

OTHER BOOKS YOU MAY ENJOY

LAST in a LONG LINE of REBELS

Lisa Lewis Tyre

PUFFIN BOOKS

PUFFIN BOOKS
An imprint of Penguin Random House LLC
375 Hudson Street
New York, New York 10014

First published in the United States of America by Nancy Paulsen Books,
an imprint of Penguin Group (USA) LLC, 2015
Published by Puffin Books, an imprint of Penguin Random House LLC, 2016

THE LIBRARY OF CONGRESS HAS CATALOGED THE NANCY PAULSEN BOOKS EDITION AS FOLLOWS:
Tyre, Lisa Lewis.
Last in a long line of rebels / Lisa Lewis Tyre.
p. cm.
Summary: When the city of Zollicoffer, Tennessee, where her family lives, announces plans to
seize their one hundred seventy-five year old house through eminent domain, twelve-year-old
Louise Mayhew needs to come up with a way to save it—and her ancestor's Civil War diary
linking the house to the Underground Railroad, as well as a hidden treasure, seem to offer her
family the best chance of saving their home.
ISBN 9780399168383 (hardcover)
[1. Underground Railroad—Tennessee—Juvenile fiction. 2. Eminent domain—Juvenile fiction.
3. Historic buildings—Juvenile fiction. 4. Families—Tennessee—Juvenile fiction.
5. Diaries—Juvenile fiction.]
I. Title.
PZ7.1.T97 Las 2015

Puffin Books ISBN 9780147512031

Printed in the United States of America

1 3 5 7 9 10 8 6 4 2

Design by Annie Ericsson

For my parents

From the diary of Louise Duncan Mayhew
September 1860

In honor of my engagement, Father has planned a Grand Celebration. The house has been painted a gleaming white, and tables, replete with wild flowers, are scattered on the lawn. The whole effect is worthy of a Charles Heath illustration and I can barely contain my excitement at the sound of approaching carriages.

Being the junkman's daughter isn't always as cool as it might sound. Sure, I get first dibs on all kinds of good stuff—I now have three perfectly good ten-speed bikes—but it comes with a price. As soon as I saw Daddy's dump truck sitting in the car line, shaking and rattling like it was about to throw a rod, I knew Sally Martin would have something snide to say. Mama usually drove me home, but Daddy had mentioned at breakfast that he had to pick up an old section of bleachers from the football field and might as well save her a trip. I could see a rusty end of it sticking up behind the cab.

"Nice ride, Louise," she said. "You headed to the dump?" A couple of kids laughed, and I calculated the chances of getting suspended for fighting on the last day of school.

Benjamin Zerto, my best friend, leaned closer and whispered, "You won't have to see her for the whole summer. Take a deep breath and count to ten." As if.

I looked at Sally and smirked. "You better stand back. My dad's used to picking up useless crap and hauling it away. You could be next."

I was rewarded with a gasp from Sally and a grin from Benzer, a win-win.

The car line moved, and I could hear the roar of the truck as it lumbered forward. Normally the car line would have been packed with kids and I'd have had some backup in addition to Benzer. But most kids had left early, as soon as they had report cards and attendance awards. Even Franklin, the brains of our group, and my cousin Patty were gone.

"I don't know how you stand it," Sally sighed. "Being surrounded by junk would be bad enough, but it looks like your house is about to fall down around your ears. My father says it's a crime to have such an eyesore right smack in the middle of town."

I rolled my eyes. My house was a common target with

Sally. I'd told her before that it looked old because it was—it had had its 175th birthday last year. I wouldn't waste my breath mentioning it again.

Sally smoothed down her skirt with one hand and smiled.

Uh-oh. When Sally smiled, bad things usually followed.

"Benzer," she said sweetly, turning to face him, "are you coming to the pool this weekend? My dad is having a cookout for all the kids." She looked at me. "All the kids in the neighborhood, I mean."

Benzer and Sally lived in the only subdivision in town, or as my grandmother called it, "the Yankee enclave." It was full of new brick homes and had a swimming pool and tennis courts with no cracks in them, unlike the ones at the city park.

"I doubt it," Benzer answered. "I'm helping Lou's dad over the weekend."

Sally pouted. "Oh, that's too bad. I guess you're going to have another boring summer. What did you write last year for your 'My Summer Vacation' essay?" She laughed. "Oh, yeah. 'Watching Paint Peel with Lou and Other Adventures in Boredom.'"

I could feel my face turning red. Last year, the essay had seemed funny. Mine had been titled "War Between the States—My Summer with a Yankee." But after hearing everyone read about going to Disney, or renting house-boats for the summer, it had felt kind of lame.

I looked for my dad. He had moved another few feet, and if all went well, I'd be sitting in his truck and riding away from this in about ninety seconds.

"That was a joke," Benzer said. "I like hanging out at Lou's. It's like something out of an R. L. Stine story."

Benzer is a bookworm, but that doesn't hurt him socially. He's the most athletic boy in the entire sixth grade. He's considered a Northerner by some, since he was born in New York City, even though he's lived here in Zollicoffer since he was four and considers himself a local. We've been best friends since kindergarten, when I sat on top of David Pinto until he promised to stop making fun of Benzer's accent.

"R. L. who?" Sally asked.

"Why don't you spend the summer reading a book?" I asked.

Sally pulled a small mirror from her backpack and checked her hair. "I'll be much too busy," she said. "We're going on a cruise in a few weeks. But I'm sure you'll have plenty of time to read while you're sitting around watching the paint peel."

Daddy pulled to the curb, and I moved to leave, but Sally's smug smile did me in. "Benzer and I have exciting plans too, Sally. Sorry you'll miss it all on your dopey cruise." I caught Benzer's startled look out of the corner of my eye, but I didn't stop. "I guess you'll hear all about it when you get back. If you don't read about it in the newspaper first."

Sally laughed. "Oh, really? I can hardly wait."

I ignored Benzer's stare and opened the dump truck's door. It gave a loud screech, and I slammed it shut. Sally murmured something to the girls around her about "Lou and her active imagination." I could hear them all laughing as we pulled away.

My first morning of summer vacation was ruined when I woke up thinking about Sally Martin. My alarm clock—the *clang-clang* sound of metal hitting metal—signaled that the scrap mountain of junk outside was getting bigger, and I looked out the window in time to see a rusty piece of tin join the pile. Great. More mess for Sally to make fun of.

Daddy inherited the house and the junk from his daddy, but he's the one who made it into a business. He said that until he got it, it was just a dump. The good things—push mowers, freezers, stoves, and so on—were in the same pile with broken toilets and rusty tin. Now we don't just pick up stuff—we resell it, too. Everything's separated into four piles: the salable, the fixable, the recyclable, and Mama's things. She's an enviro artist, which means she welds the junk together and makes a bigger pile called "art."

I was in my bedroom lying on one of the fixables, a

cast-iron bed Daddy had welded back together, when Mama called me down to breakfast. I lay there listening to the sounds from below. I pictured my pregnant Mama standing at the stove cooking grits, her tummy so big she had to stretch her arm almost straight to stir. Bertie, my grandmother, would be sitting at the table drinking coffee, gossiping, and complaining how "Yankees are just every-where I turn nowadays." She's always saying that even though Yankees like to move to Tennessee, they don't tend to stay long. They think things will be simpler, but when they find out the truth, they race out of town as fast as their SUVs will take them.

Bertie claimed she moved in to help Mama with the baby preparations, and everyone went along with that. It wasn't true, but I've learned that a lot of what we pretend about people usually isn't.

I changed quickly, picking up an old pair of gym shorts off the floor, and a University of Tennessee T-shirt that read 1998 NATIONAL CHAMPIONS from under the bed. Barefoot, I headed down the stairs.

"Morning, sugar," Mama said. She turned to hug me as I entered the kitchen. With her belly in the way, I ended up more or less under her armpit.

"Morning," I said, and hurriedly sat at the table. I'd learned she was pregnant months ago, but it still gave me the heebie-jeebies. Mama was in this weird stage where she constantly put my hand on her belly and made me feel the baby kick. She swore it could hear my voice. It wasn't even born yet, and already it was listening in on my conversations.

"How's it going, kid?" Bertie asked from her seat at the scarred oak table. Even though it was barely eight o'clock, she was dressed in white pants, a red blouse tied at the waist, and full makeup.

I combed my fingers through my hair, wincing as they caught in the tangles.

"Fine."

Bertie gestured to the empty seat beside her. She sipped from her BORN TO PARTY—FORCED TO WORK mug. "Fine? Girl, what I'd give to be twelve again. I'd hallelujah the county!"

Mama put a plate of biscuits on the table. "The world could not take you going through puberty again, Mother. Besides, it's probably not as good as you remember it. I read on the Internet that thirty-nine percent of teenagers suffer from stress."

"Oh, Lord, not this Internet thing again," Bertie said.

I stuffed a biscuit into my mouth to keep from laughing. At least once a month, we have a "family meeting" over some issue Mama read about on the computer. Last month was about how inhaling household cleaners could kill. Before that it was teenage runaways. Just hearing the words *family meeting* made my heart beat faster. They also used them to tell me about things like the pregnancy, Bertie moving in to help with the baby, and Aunt Sophie's divorce. But they never told me the important stuff—like why.

Thankfully, my house had all kinds of places to hide; otherwise, I'd never have known anything. I was reading in the broom closet under the stairs when I found out that Bertie was really living with us because her third husband, the dentist, had maxed out all of her credit cards, leaving her with nothing but a pile of debt and a brand-new set of veneers. And I'd been in the secret closet across from my parents' bedroom when I heard that the dentist, now Bertie's ex-husband, had gone and married their next-door neighbor, Thelma Johnson, and was "living it up right across town."

"Lou, I swear people must think that University of Tennessee shirt is the only thing you own," Mama said. "You're going to have to take it off and let me wash it before it walks in here by itself."

I leaned my head down and gave it a sniff. "Still smells good to me. But, hey, speaking of UT, have you given any more thought to the baby's name?"

Mama put both hands on her hips. "I am *not* naming this child Peyton!"

"But, Mama, it works for—"

"Both a boy and a girl," Mama and Bertie finished together.

"I don't care," Mama said. "I'm not naming this child after a football player no one will remember in five years."

I swooned dramatically in my chair. "Are you kidding me? Peyton Manning's going to make history! I can't believe you would even say that!"

The back door opened, and Isaac Coleman stuck his head in. "They giving you a hard time already, Lou?"

Mama waved him into the kitchen. "Giving *her* a hard time? I'm the one getting another pitch for naming the baby Peyton. If you have a minute, I'll fix you some sausage biscuits."

"Thank you." He winked at me. "For the record, I like Peyton as a name. Of course, I also like John, Terrell, and Rod."

"Are those family names?" Mama asked.

I laughed. "Isaac's going to name his kids after the Broncos lineup. That's John as in Elway, Terrell Davis, and Rod Smith."

"Oh, you two with your football references," Mama said. She pointed a spoon at Isaac. "Now, you're not planning on getting married anytime soon, are you?"

That wiped the grin off Isaac's face. "No way. I'm not even thinking about that until after college. Way after college."

Mama put the platter on the table, and Bertie pulled out a chair. "Have a seat and eat. Nothing I like better than breakfast with a handsome young man."

I rolled my eyes. Bertie was a flirt and a half, but I couldn't really blame her. Isaac *was* handsome. He had dark eyes and skin the color of Mama's coffee after she added a tiny bit of cream. Plus he was super smart and the best defensive end this town had ever seen.

He'd been helping Daddy in the junkyard since he was a freshman, so he was practically family. He had just graduated a couple of days before, and I was going to miss him like crazy when he left for college.

"What's wrong, Lou?" Bertie asked. "You look like someone just snapped your garter."

"Nothing. Just thinking."

She smiled. "Well, don't make it look like such a struggle."

"What are you doing today?" Isaac asked.

I shrugged. "Not sure. Benzer's coming over to hang out."

"Doesn't he get enough of that working on Saturdays?"

"I guess not. Besides, we're going to make a plan."

"A plan?" Bertie asked. "That sounds ominous."

"We're trying to think of something exciting to do this summer. Hey, Jackson Parker's parents rented a houseboat last year." I looked at Mama. "Does Daddy know anybody at the lake?"

"Right." Mama brushed her hair off her forehead. "That's how I want to spend the last weeks of this pregnancy, in a bathing suit!"

Bertie laughed. "Why do you want excitement, anyway? That's a Northerner's invention."

I grinned. "You mean like the lightbulb and auto-mobiles?"

Mama put an arm around my shoulders. "You've got to get up pretty early to get one over on Lou, Mother."

"Lord, don't I know it. That girl is sharp as a tack." Bertie winked. "I like to think she gets it from me."

Benzer threw an old basketball against my house. Tiny white flakes fell and drifted down with every thump.

"So we just have to come up with something exciting to do this summer. How hard could it be?" he asked.

I blew a dandelion and watched the wind carry the fluff across the yard. "Impossible. Nothing exciting ever happens around here. We haven't even had a decent fire since the courthouse burned, and that was over a hundred years ago!"

He shook his dark hair out of his eyes and threw the ball again. This time he aimed toward a bicycle rim Daddy had nailed on the light pole in the front yard. *Thwack!* "Who cares what Sally thinks anyway?"

I sighed. Sally had been teasing me throughout elementary school. I was going to try to not let her ruin junior high for me too. "I do. Face it, we need a miracle."

A car pulled into the library across the street, and Mrs. Ray from the Five and Dime store waved at us as she got out. One of the best things about my home is how close it is to everything. I can walk to the square, the library, the museum, the town pool, the baseball field, and even the junior high.

I turned over and lay flat on the grass, looking at my house. The windows on the bottom floor were open, and the living room curtains moved in and out of the windows with the breeze. It felt like the house was breathing. There were four columns running across the front of the house, two of which had termite damage, and the porch seemed to sag a bit on one side, but for a house that was almost two hundred years old, I thought it looked okay. Sally's eyesore comment bugged me. A few years ago, the city made a regulation to prevent unsightly areas within the city limits, but Daddy said we were "grandfathered in." I had thought that meant since my grandfather started the junkyard, we didn't have to change, but it was more like that we were here before the regulation, so they couldn't bother us. Daddy had enclosed the backyard with a fence, just to be neighborly, but it didn't take long for the junk to tower over it.

Benzer fell down next to me. "Why are you frowning?"

"Do you think the house looks bad? Be honest."

"Not bad," he said. "It looks old, but that just gives it character."

"That's one word for it."

I'm the latest in a long line of Mayhews that have lived here, and every one of them has added on in some way. The house is three stories, and Daddy says that the sunroom was probably added later, as was the large utility room off of the kitchen. His grandfather supposedly thought the house looked unbalanced, so he added more bedrooms on each side. Now the second floor has a total of four bedrooms, counting Bertie's, which used to be an upstairs parlor. It looks like a mess of rooms and random columns attached to nothing, all held together by overgrown grapevines, but it's ours.

Benzer pushed himself up on his elbows. "I know something exciting. You could go with me to the park and watch me hit balls over the fence. What could be better than that?"

"Absolutely anything?"

"You're in a great mood. Does your mom have any colas in the fridge? It's burning up out here."

"Oh, come on." I climbed to my feet. "Mama's on an organic juice kick right now, but I know where Bertie keeps her stash."

We brushed the grass from our clothes and walked to the porch. The front door was open to let in the breeze, and I stood in the doorway letting my eyes adjust to the dimness. The living room was just off the foyer, and I motioned Benzer inside. "Wait here. I'll check if they're out of the kitchen."

I walked down the hallway. Mama's and Bertie's voices drifted up from the cellar. Satisfied, I walked back to Benzer. "It should be okay. They're down in the cellar looking through my old baby clothes. That'll take hours."

Benzer was on his knees in front of the bookcase, a large, dusty Bible in his lap.

"What are you doing?" I asked.

"I haven't seen this in forever. Not since your mother banned us from ever touching it again."

I sat down beside him. "Oh, yeah. But it was Bertie's fault for telling us if we prayed for something with a sincere heart, we'd get it." A smile snuck across my face. "Remember, I asked for it to snow?"

Benzer laughed. "That's right, in August. When it didn't, you threw the Bible across the room."

"I *dropped* it. How old were we, seven?" I opened the cover and read, "*Universal Library of Divine Knowledge, containing the sacred texts of the Old and New Testaments, in which the important truths are confirmed to dispel the mists of darkness, enlighten the ignorant, and implant divine knowledge which is necessary to salvation.*"

"Wow," Benzer said, "that ought to cover it."

"I don't know what half of that means." I traced a finger across the penciled name at the top. "*Silas Whittle, 1858.*"

"Who was that?"

"I'm not sure. Somebody in the family, I guess."

Benzer picked up my hand and placed it on a page with a drawing of a baby Jesus. "What are you waiting for?"

"What do you mean?" I asked.

"Try again. You just said we need a miracle. Ask it for something exciting."

"Whatever. It didn't snow, remember?" I wiped my dusty hand on my shorts.

"Do you have a better idea?"

I pictured Sally's smirking face as we stood on the sidewalk in front of school. "Fine, but why do I have to say it?"

"You're the one who told Sally we had big plans. And it's your family Bible—duh!"

I exhaled slowly. "Okay. What should I say?"

"I don't know. Just ask for something exciting to happen, sincerely. Then offer to do something God likes."

"Hello? How do I know what God likes? You're the one with a cross above your couch."

"We're Catholic. All I know for sure is that he likes the pope."

"You're a big help." I closed my eyes, feeling silly. "Uh . . . Lord, I know I haven't talked to you much, or ever, to be honest. But I've seen the pope on TV, and he looks like a nice guy. I like his car." I paused. This was not going well. "Anyway, we'd like to ask, sincerely, if you could give us a summer with some excitement. Could you please make something happen, something life-changing, so that when we go to junior high this fall, we're the talk of the school? And to show our sincere hearts, we'll . . ." I drew a blank.

"Hurry," Benzer whispered.

"What can we do?" I whispered back. "You think of something!"

"And to show our sincere hearts," Benzer said, "we'll start going to church. Thank you very much."

"Church? That's all you could think of?" I slammed the book shut. "Amen."

A huge gust of wind came through the open window. It ruffled my hair, and I could see the oak leaves on my tree outside fluttering wildly. The curtains were sucked outside, then pushed back into the room, just in time for the window to drop with a loud *BANG*.

"What the heck?" Benzer asked.

"Lou, is that you?" Mama called from the cellar. "What are you doing up there?"

Quickly, I tried to stuff the Bible back on the bookshelf, but the cover caught on a small nail sticking out of the wood and tore.

Benzer and I stared at each other, panicked.

"Lou?" Mama's voice was getting louder, and I heard the door at the top of the cellar stairs open.

"C'mon," I whispered to Benzer.

Of all the hiding places in my house, the one I used most was the one behind the living room bookcase. Daddy said it was probably used in the Civil War to hide valuables. I tugged on the edge of the shelf. The wood floor underneath was worn to a high shine, and it swung forward easily.

I grabbed Benzer's arm and pushed him into the dark space ahead of me. On the inside, a leather cord was attached with a nail. I pulled the bookcase shut, plunging us into darkness.

"We're going to be grounded for life," Benzer whispered in the dark.

"Shh." I got on my knees and felt around the floor. "Aha." I clicked the On button of the flashlight I'd found. "I like to read in here when cleaning's going on," I whispered.

"Lou? Benzer?" Mama's voice was loud in the room. "Are you here?"

I aimed the light at Benzer, who crossed his eyes and stuck out his tongue. I tried not to laugh.

The floor vibrated as someone with a heavier tread walked into the room. "What's going on?" Daddy asked.

"Did you see Lou and Benzer outside?" Mama asked. "I swear I heard something fall."

"No, but remind them I need them to work early tomorrow."

The sofa nearest the bookcase groaned with the weight of someone sitting down. Great, it looked like we were going to be stuck here awhile.

"Where's Bertie?" Daddy asked. I heard a soft thump, and I pictured him dropping his work boots onto the floor.

"Pulling out some of Lou's old clothes for the baby."

"You better sit down," Daddy said. "I've got bad news."

"Oh, dear. What is it?"

"I just got a call from Jimmy Dale. Pete got the votes

he needed. He's already submitted a plan and everything." Daddy sounded tired. "Things are moving ahead."

Benzer raised an eyebrow. "What are they talking about?" he whispered.

I shook my head. I didn't have a clue.

"Are you sure Jimmy heard right?" Mama asked. "You know how things get twisted around in this town."

"Not this time. He was there when it went to the vote." The couch groaned as Daddy moved again. "I hate to say it, Lily, but we have to face facts. If Pete Winningham gets his way, this house will be history before the summer's out."

I gasped so loud I was afraid I'd given us away. Benzer nudged me with his elbow, his eyes wide in the flashlight's glare.

"I don't understand. Jimmy said the majority were voting our way. He assured us!" My mother's voice cracked on the last note.

"I guess a couple of people must have changed their minds at the last second."

I could hear Mama start to cry. I turned the flashlight off and put my knuckle in my mouth. I was glad Benzer couldn't see my face.

"Lily, please don't worry," I heard Daddy say. "We knew this might happen. That's why I spoke with those Knoxville attorneys. They've already agreed to take the case if it comes down to it."

"But they said there were no guarantees we'd win, and

they won't even start without the retainer. Where are we going to get twenty-five thousand dollars?"

I fanned my face with one hand. The tiny room was getting hot.

"I've got some things in the shop ready for the Nashville flea market," Daddy said. "We'll clean up the yard and sell everything that's worth anything."

Mama was quiet. I guessed she was calculating what all those rusty refrigerators were really worth. We just sold Mr. Otto from Sparta three of the better ones for two hundred dollars, and that was a good deal. I must have been right, because a second later, she started crying again.

"Lily, you know we've been in tough spots before. We'll figure something out. We always do."

Mama blew her nose. "I reckon you're right. I still have some art to send out. Maybe I'll find a rich buyer."

Daddy paused. Mama's art sales had never even covered the cost of her paintbrushes. "We'll talk about it tonight. Lou's bound to be back soon."

"Lord, don't let her find out. She'd plan an assault on the county."

He laughed, a short, sharp bark. "That'll be plan B. C'mon now. Is lunch ready? I've never had a problem that your chicken salad couldn't fix."

We sat in the darkness, listening to them leave.

"Lou," Benzer whispered, "we should get out while they're in the kitchen."

I put a shaking hand on the bookcase and pushed it open. Light spilled in, and I saw Benzer's face, serious and sad. I wondered if mine looked as bad as his.

We closed the bookcase, and I put the Bible back on the shelf, then we tiptoed to the front door.

I didn't trust myself to speak until we'd cleared the porch and walked around the yard, through the wooden gate, and into the junkyard. Luckily, no customers were around. I stopped in the shade of the scrap metal pile.

"Lou? Are you okay?" Benzer asked.

It suddenly occurred to me I should sit down before my legs gave way. I plopped in the dirt.

"Lou?" Benzer said again, softly. "What are you going to do?"

I looked around me at the junk piled everywhere. The back of my house was visible over the wooden fence, and over the roof of my house the top of the old oak that brushed against my window and kept me up at night. I tried to imagine the house gone, knocked down and carted off in dump trucks like the one we owned.

I shook my head and answered honestly. "I don't know yet." But one thing was for sure, I was not about to sit around and let this all become history.

CHAPTER 2

From the diary of Louise Duncan Mayhew
January 1861

Father has gone again, this time to Nashville to stay with friends and gather news about our possible secession. Although Walter's family owns no slaves, he agrees that secession is the route Tennessee must also take. He speaks of tariffs and taxes. I confess much of it goes right over my head.

Weekends are Daddy's busiest time, due to all of the yard sales and auctions. Our town doesn't have a Goodwill or Salvation Army store, so we get called to pick up anything that's not sold.

"You ready to go, Chief?" Daddy asked as he started the truck. The engine roared to life, vibrating the cab and causing old Vienna sausage cans and empty chip bags to dance across the floorboard.

"Ready!" Breakfast had been interesting. My parents

had laughed and teased like they didn't have a care in the world. I wondered how they got so good at hiding things.

"Do you have the directions?" Daddy asked.

I nodded and held up a worn notebook.

I'm the official navigator. Zollicoffer itself doesn't have a lot of people, but Grey County is one of the largest in Tennessee. Nobody uses street names; they just leave messages on the phone like "take the bypass, pass the convenience store, and turn left at the grove of pine trees."

Isaac normally helped, but he had family in town, so Daddy insisted he take the day off. There'd been an award ceremony at the bank the night before, where they had given away the annual Pride of Zollicoffer scholarship, and I thought Isaac was a shoo-in to win.

"Do you think the paper sent a photographer to the award ceremony?" I asked. "I want to see what Isaac's face looked like when they called his name."

"Probably."

I turned to look at him. "Why does your voice sound weird?"

He shrugged. "Let's just say I'll feel better once I know Isaac actually won."

"Daddy! Of course he won. It's guaranteed!"

He smiled. "I'm old enough to know nothing is guaranteed and not to count your chickens before they hatch. But you're probably right. As soon as we hear, you can start leading the charge to erect an Isaac statue in the middle of town."

"Deal!"

We drove through town, stopping at Betty Sim's house for an old air conditioner, two broken stools, and a box of clothes, size twenty. Betty had recently joined Weight Watchers, and it was paying off. You can tell a lot about a person from her garbage.

There were several more stops, mostly unexciting, except for a box of *Seventeen* magazines from Tracy Kimmel's house. My friend, her brother, Franklin, was standing in the driveway.

Daddy rested his elbow on the edge of the door. "Look who it is—Zollicoffer's own Bobby Fischer."

I stared at my dad, confused. "Who the heck is that?"

Franklin tossed a bag of trash over the side. "Bobby Fischer is considered by some to be the greatest chess player that ever lived."

"Do you even play chess?"

Franklin threw another bag. "I have a working knowledge of the game, but I believe your father was referring more to the intellectual pursuit than any real skill I might have."

Daddy laughed. "Franklin, I swear you beat all. You're probably going to be the governor of Tennessee one of these days."

Franklin turned pink. "Thank you, Mr. Mayhew. It's one of my five long-term goals."

"I tried calling you all night last night," I said.

"I'm sorry. Tracy and I drove our parents to the airport, and we didn't get home until late."

"Are they going to be gone long?" Daddy asked.

Franklin shook his head. "No, sir, just two weeks. Our grandmother is coming to stay with us."

"Well, call us if you need anything, Franklin," Daddy said in his serious voice. "I know you're the smartest twelve-year-old this town has ever seen, but everyone needs help now and then."

Franklin peered up from under his glasses. "Thank you, but I'm sure we'll be fine. I'll see you tonight, Lou."

We waved bye and started down the long, tree-lined driveway. Mr. and Mrs. Kimmel were the richest people in Zollicoffer and were constantly heading off on cruises or vacations to Europe. Tracy, Franklin's perfect and popular sister, was a cheerleader and last year's Homecoming Queen. Her sweet sixteen party had been written up in the Nashville *Tennessean* . . . most of it, anyway. Franklin gave us the secret details—like that the seniors got grounded for drinking spiked punch and puking in his mother's flower beds. Not that he was invited; he'd watched it all from his upstairs window.

Next we went to pick up Benzer. He lives in the only subdivision in town because his parents say they feel more comfortable with people around. They're the only family I know that keep their doors locked in the daytime.

Benzer has to mow the yard every Saturday before he can work at the junkyard. Normally he walks the half mile to our house, but since Daddy needed our help at an auction, we said we'd pick him up. He was sitting on the front stoop, grass clippings clinging to his tennis shoes, trimming his nails with a pocketknife when we pulled to the curb.

"Morning, Benzini. You ready to work?" my dad asked.

"Yes, sir." He opened the truck door. "What'd I miss?"

"Nothing much," I said, scooting over on the bench seat to give him room. "Some fashion magazines from Tracy Kimmel's."

He made a gagging sound and mimed throwing up out the window.

"Before I forget, Mr. Mayhew," Benzer said. "Dad wanted me to tell you that he could use a good computer if you come across any."

"I might have one or two in the shop," Daddy said over the hum of the engine. "I'll test them out over the weekend and see what I can find. You guys ready for a burger?"

I nodded. It was barely eleven, but we'd been up since dawn. We pulled into the parking lot of Dixie's Burgers.

"I'll be right back. Y'all want the usual?"

We nodded, and he shut the door.

"So, find out anything new?" Benzer asked. He smelled like soap, and his hair was drying into curly, dark flips around his collar. Had it always been that thick? I slid across into Daddy's seat.

"Not really. I looked online and found out 'Pete' is Peter Winningham, county commissioner. But there was nothing about him that would explain why he'd want to steal my house."

"I think that's Blake Winningham's dad. I've seen him at Little League games. Blake stinks, by the way."

"That's helpful." I could see Daddy at the counter giving our order. "The whole thing is just so weird. Why would anyone want our house?"

"Good question." Benzer began playing drums on the dashboard. "I hope he remembers to get extra ketchup."

"You always say that, and he always does. What am I supposed to do?"

"Why don't you just ask your parents what's going on? Or Bertie. I bet she knows."

"Right. I'll just tell them we were eavesdropping. They'll probably only ground me until school starts. That will really show Sally Martin."

"That's it!" Benzer smacked the dashboard. "Lou, we prayed for an exciting summer. The prayer is already working!"

I frowned. "This is not what I call exciting."

Benzer shrugged. "Well, it's not exactly boring, either. We weren't real specific about the kind of excitement."

I rubbed my eyes. I didn't care why it was happening. I just wanted to know how to fix it.

"Did you tell Franklin?" Benzer asked. "If anyone will know how to handle this, it will be him."

"I couldn't say anything with Daddy there," I said. "I'll tell him and Patty about it tonight. You're coming, aren't you?"

Daddy came out carrying two bags, and I scooted back next to Benzer.

He nodded. "Right after ball practice."

Daddy drove to the city park, pulled under the canopy of a large tree, and turned off the engine.

"We've got thirty minutes before we need to be at the auction," he explained.

Local auctioneers hire Daddy to remove anything left over from their sales. We take the stuff home and then appliances are repaired and sold to vendors in Cookeville or Monterey; furniture is stripped, painted, and resold. The best money is in scrap metal.

I went through the bags and handed out burgers, onion rings, and little packets of ketchup.

"Hey, Mr. Mayhew," Benzer said, tearing the wrapper off his burger, "you think we'll get anything good today?"

Daddy winked. "You know, Benzer, I've got a feeling we just might."

"That's right," I piped in. "Daddy says Mr. Wilson is from the Chandler Wilson line. Civil War descendants."

"Or the War Between the States, as your grandmother likes to call it," Daddy said.

Benzer shook his head as if to clear it. "What you're saying is this was an old geezer with a lifetime of junk?"

"Exactly," Daddy answered.

"Daddy," I said, "why didn't you and Mr. Wilson like each other?"

He looked surprised. "What makes you say that?"

"Last night Bertie said he's probably having a heart attack in Hades 'cause you might make a buck off his stuff."

"Oh, just old family animosity. It's ancient history, really."

Benzer leaned forward. "What happened? Did somebody run off with his wife?"

Daddy laughed. "Nothing like that." He paused, taking a long sip of his cola. "Years ago, the Mayhews owned a lot more land than what you see now. It was all pastures and woods back then, of course. After the war, our family had to sell off just about everything—the horses, most of the land and livestock. The worst part, though, was selling family heirlooms. Guess who bought most of that?"

"The Wilson family!" I said.

"That's right."

"What happened?" Benzer asked.

Daddy wiped his mouth with a napkin. "Times were

tough, I reckon. When Louise Mayhew died, her son sold off some stuff. Families do what they have to do. It probably wasn't too different from the auction we're going to today."

"I've never heard this story. Was Louise the one I was named after?"

"That's the one."

I was puzzled. "If they held an auction, why didn't they sell the house?"

"The family sold most everything, but not that," Daddy said, a grim line to his mouth. "Somehow, we managed to hang on to that."

He didn't say it, but the phrase "so far" hung in the air.

The Wilson property was about eight miles from town. We parked in an open field next to several rows of cars.

"I'll get some boys to help with the heavy stuff," Daddy said, jumping down from the truck. "Y'all make yourselves useful."

We spent the next hour running back and forth between the house and Daddy's truck. We had to wait for Daddy and the auction workers to load a beat-up freezer and a dryer missing its door before we could start throwing the smaller stuff in the back.

My arms felt like cooked noodles.

"Do you see anything else?" Benzer asked.

"I don't think so. We better ask."

We found Mr. Tate, the auctioneer, going through receipts with an odd-looking man in black-rimmed glasses. He was wearing a suit, even though it was already sweltering, and a gold pocket watch peeked out of his vest.

"Are you sure that's everything?" I heard him ask.

Mr. Tate shrugged. "That's everything the family authorized us to sell. You might talk with them if you're looking for something specific."

The man shook his head. "No, that's not necessary. I was just checking."

Noticing us, Mr. Tate gestured to the side of the house. "Lou, there's a few pieces of junk down in the cellar. If you and Benzer can grab that, you'll be done."

We could smell the mold as soon as we opened the door.

"Yuck," I said, putting a hand over my nose.

Benzer pulled his T-shirt up over half his face. "Hurry." He led the way down a set of rickety stairs.

An old wooden box, covered in cobwebs, stood in the corner. We picked it up and piled a toaster, four moldy books, two stained lampshades, and a chipped shovel inside it. Working together, we were able to carry it up the stairs, out of the house, and into the sunlight.

"Whew," Benzer said, "that was nasty."

I bent down and looked at the box. "This is kind of cool."

Even painted a marine green and covered with mildew, there was something pretty about it. One of the iron hinges was missing from the top, and both handles were broken, but otherwise the box seemed in good condition. A carved border ran the length of the wood.

"Hey," Benzer said, running his hand across the surface, "these look like birds."

"Y'all ready?" Daddy asked, walking toward the truck. He was frowning, and I wondered if Mr. Tate had tried to avoid paying.

"As soon as we put this on the truck," Benzer answered.

I helped clear a spot in the truck bed. "Hey, Daddy. Can I keep this box?"

"Sure," he answered without looking at me. "You know the rule—workers get first dibs."

Daddy was still frowning, and Benzer shot me a puzzled look.

"Is everything okay, Daddy?"

"Not really, ace. Mr. Tate just told me that Isaac didn't win last night, and I know he needed a scholarship of that size to afford UT, where he was really hoping to go. But the coach gave it to the Canton boy."

"Drew Canton?" Benzer asked. "He's not nearly as good as Isaac."

"Well, according to Coach Peeler he is. Stupid son of a—uh, gun."

"But everybody knows Isaac is the best!" I said, jumping down from the back. "He even broke a school record last year."

Daddy opened the truck's door and sighed. "Let's get going."

I crawled in and leaned against the cracked upholstery. Daddy started the truck and pulled out of the parking area. He looked like he was as bummed as I was.

"But, Daddy," I said, "why would Coach Peeler give the scholarship to Drew Canton and not Isaac?"

"Well, I'm guessing he'd probably say that Drew was more involved in civic stuff, as well as having good grades. The scholarship is actually based on more than just athletics."

"What do you mean, 'civic stuff'?" Benzer asked.

"Community service, volunteering, that sort of thing. I've seen Drew's truck parked at the food pantry every now and then."

I stomped the floorboard. "But that's not fair. Isaac has to work on Saturdays."

"These things are subjective, Lou. Do you know what that means?"

I shook my head. "Not really."

"It means something is based on perspective, not cold, hard facts. It's like the difference between judging a beauty contest versus a bike race. A bike race is the first person across the finish line, but a beauty contest would depend on who was judging and what they considered good-looking. See?"

"I guess so. So you think Coach Peeler gave Drew the scholarship because he volunteers more than Isaac?"

"No, I don't think it's that simple." Daddy let out a long breath. "I've known Coach Peeler since I was in high school. I wouldn't say this about just anybody, but he had a reputation." He stopped the truck in front of Benzer's house.

"A reputation?" I asked. "What kind of reputation?"

Daddy's mouth turned down at the corners. "For treating blacks differently."

"What?" I asked. "You mean he didn't pick Isaac because he's black?"

"I think so," Daddy said.

"But that's ridiculous! Who thinks like that? It's 1999 for crying out loud!" I said.

"Wow. Isn't there anything Isaac can do?" Benzer asked. "Can't he sue or something?"

"Maybe, but it might be hard to prove, and it would cost his family a lot to fight," Daddy said. "I'll have a talk with Isaac and see what he's thinking. I'm sure he's disappointed, but he probably knew it was a possibility."

"This really stinks," I said.

"I know." Daddy fished a bill out of his wallet and handed it to Benzer.

Benzer opened the door and jumped out. "I'll see you later, Lou. Thanks, Mr. Mayhew."

I slumped down and avoided talking the rest of the ride home. Daddy pulled into our driveway and turned off the truck.

"I'll put your box in the shop. Let me know if we're out of stain. I think that old dresser we fixed up used most of it."

"Okay. I better go help Mama get ready for tonight."

"Hey, don't forget your money," he said.

I stuffed the cash into my back pocket. "Thanks."

He put a hand on my arm. "You know I'm proud of you, right?"

I attempted to smile. "I know."

Daddy leaned forward to put his wallet in his back pocket. "You're going to make a good big sister."

I jumped down from the truck. The way my luck was going, Mama would have twins!

I spent the rest of the afternoon helping Mama clean the house. Normally I would have complained, but since learning we might have to move, things seemed somehow different. Instead of thinking about how hard it was to mop the wooden floors, I noticed what a nice shade of caramel they were. In fact, I noticed all sorts of things I'd seen but never really thought about, like how the windows had counterweights attached so they'd stay up and how pretty the glass doorknobs were.

"Bertie and I are walking to Upchurch's to get some snacks for tonight," Mama said. "You want to come?"

I shook my head. "You guys go ahead. I'm beat."

I watched them from the parlor window until they were two blocks away, then I went over to the bookshelf and pulled out the Bible.

The hole I'd torn in the cover stared at me like an accusing eye. I flipped the pages until I found the same picture of baby Jesus, and put my hand across it. "God, sorry about that last prayer. Can we just say never mind? I'll still go to church and all, but if you wanted to just forget the excitement part, that'd be great. Amen."

I opened my eyes. Last time the wind had blown so hard the window fell, but this time, all was quiet. "Bummer."

I flipped through the pages absentmindedly, and they gaped open toward the back of the Bible, where a thin envelope was wedged deep inside. Across the top were the words *Confederate States of America*.

"What the heck?" I opened the envelope and pulled out a handwritten letter. The script was spindly and hard to read, and I struggled to make sense of it.

March 12, 1864

Dear Louise,

I received your kind letter a few days ago. I was glad to hear that you are fareing well despite the circumstances. Mrs. Reagan is indeed a true friend but her kindness to you

is a credit to your own charm and goodness.
I pray you will remane well until I am home,
which I am hopeful will be soon. As to the
other matter you referenced, I indicated at
our last meeting that my feelings on the issue
have quite changed, but I urge you to be
caushus my dear Louise, as reports are that
the enemy is nearby. Your bravery in the midst
of all that has transpired and the memorey
of your sweet smile carries me through these
long nites.

> *Your love,*
> *WLM*

I didn't know who WLM was, but he wouldn't have passed fifth-grade spelling. And this was the second time today I was hearing about my namesake, Louise, which was strange and exciting.

I read the letter once more before slipping it back into the Bible.

The letter mentioned Louise's bravery. Well, that was something. I could only hope that some of it had been passed down to me.

CHAPTER 3

From the diary of Louise Duncan Mayhew
April 1861

Mother attempts normality through garden parties and hosting friends for whist, but the men are on fire with talk of war. Tennessee has rejected secession, though the vote in Nashville proved what everyone feared, that Tennessee is divided in its stance on secession. East Tennessee supports staying in the Union, while people in the western part of the state are against. Here in the middle, we're just as divided. Yesterday, while shopping, Mrs. Nolan Paul pointedly ignored me. I glared at her back in a way that I hoped would raise blisters. A friendship lost because my betrothed and I support secession.

Patty was the first to arrive, all decked out in a black sundress with matching black sandals. With her skinny frame and red hair, I thought she looked like a matchstick.

Aunt Sophie jumped out of the car and ran past where I sat on the front porch. "Sorry, Lou, but I drank a large glass of sweet tea, and I'm about to wet myself."

"Mother!" Patty shook her head, causing curls to bounce. "What if Franklin and Benzer were here?"

"I'm sure they have bodily functions too, dear." Aunt Sophie closed the front door behind her.

"She's trying to make me crazy. Oh!" Patty threw herself down on the steps next to me. "Speaking of crazy, Sally Martin's been telling tales about you. She said you were bragging about how you've got awesome summer plans. What's up with that?"

I groaned. "Great. I should have known she'd tell everybody in the state what I said. If gossip was an Olympic sport, she'd win the gold medal."

"I can't believe you told her that. Sally already tries to make your life miserable. Now she'll have more ammunition when school starts and you haven't done anything . . ." Patty shook her head and poked me. "Maybe you can be homeschooled."

A car honked, announcing that Mrs. Kimmel had arrived. Franklin's grandmother had been Bertie's bridge partner for years. My earliest memories of Franklin were of us playing on the floor beneath their card table. Now the two women were trying hard to teach Mama and Aunt Sophie, because, as Bertie said, "We need some young blood. Everybody our age keeps dying on us."

Franklin climbed out of the backseat just as Benzer, wearing an old baseball uniform and covered in dirt, walked into the yard.

Bertie opened the front door and stood at the porch railing. "Finally, the whole gang's here."

Patty and I stood to let Mrs. Kimmel pass, then sank back down on the porch steps. Benzer and Franklin sat down cross-legged on the grass in front of us.

"Have you told them yet?" Benzer asked.

I shook my head. As much as I wanted to tell them about the house, just saying it out loud made it somehow worse. I rested my chin on my knees. "You tell it."

Patty looked from me to Benzer. "What? Somebody tell it, whatever it is, before I go nuts."

Benzer leaned forward and began to tell them the story, from the praying over the Bible to the part where we overheard my parents talking about the house being demolished.

Patty only interrupted once. "You two were hiding behind the bookshelf? Is that something you do a lot?"

"No! I just didn't want to get caught holding a ripped Bible," I said. "Besides, that's kinda not the point of the story."

Franklin pulled a small book out of his back pocket and rolled it into a tight spiral. He tapped it against his chin, looking off into the yard.

"Oh, Lord, Franklin's in his thinking pose," Patty said.

Franklin ignored her. "Did you hear them say how they were going to take the house?" he asked. "Perhaps you're breaking a city ordinance, or a code, with the junkyard?"

"No, we went through all that a couple of years ago," I said. "Daddy said they'd had a vote, and it could be demolished by the end of the summer." My voice sounded funny, and I cleared my throat.

"Hmmm."

"What are you thinking?" Benzer asked. "Is there a way out of this?"

Franklin dropped his book on the concrete in front of him. "I'm not sure. There are only three reasons that I can think of that would result in Lou losing her home. Of course, there could be others that I don't know, but three main reasons."

"Oh, get on with it, Professor," Patty snapped.

Franklin held up a finger. "One, nonpayment of some kind—mortgage, taxes, et cetera. But that would be a bank issue, or perhaps a government issue, not something people would vote on." He held up a second finger. "Number two would be if the property had become uninhabitable or dangerous. Black mold or a fire that had made the home too dangerous to live in, for example." He looked around the house. "I guess that's not it?"

"We don't have mold, Franklin, geesh."

"Well, it might be better if you did. Mold can be removed. Since we've ruled out the first two"—he held up a third finger—"then I would say that your home is being threatened by eminent domain."

"Eminent what?" I asked.

"Eminent domain. It lets the government seize private property without the owner's consent for government use—roadways, civic buildings, power lines, and so on. It's actually very broad."

"Dude," Benzer said. "Tell me you're making that up."

Franklin shook his head. "It's really quite common. It's how many of our state parks were formed."

I could feel anger growing like a mushroom cloud inside of my chest. "You mean that they can just decide they want your land and make you move? That's horrible!"

"Well, they do have to pay you a fair price."

"What if you don't want to sell it for any price?" I asked.

Franklin frowned. "Then they can go to court and get it condemned."

Benzer looked around the yard. "I wonder what they're planning on using it for."

"It is a prime location," Franklin said. "There are not a lot of homes on this much land in the middle of town. I'll look on the city website when I get home. If they had a vote, there'll be a record of the meeting somewhere."

Patty leaned her thin shoulder into mine. "So what are you going to do? What's the plan?"

"Plan? There's no plan! What can I do? You heard

Franklin, if the government wants your house, they can take it!" I was so frustrated I wanted to scream. I jumped to my feet, accidentally kicking Franklin's book across the yard. "By the end of the summer, I'll be homeless, and there's nothing I can do about it." I stormed over to the oak tree. A small branch had fallen, and I picked it up and threw it toward the ditch near the street. "This stinks."

Franklin and Benzer studied their shoes, avoiding my eyes. I looked at Patty, expecting her to be angry, but she just looked sad. "It's not the worst thing, Lou. You wouldn't be homeless, really. Franklin said they had to pay you, so y'all would have money to buy somewhere good, maybe even in Benzer's subdivision."

"You don't understand," I mumbled. "I can't move." I dropped back down on the steps. "Franklin, you're the smartest kid in school and the richest. Benzer, you're the best athlete, the bookworm, the kid from New York; there's nobody like you at school. Patty . . ." I hesitated, trying to find the right words. "You've got that whole fashionista thing going. Even high-school girls ask you for hair tips."

Patty sniffed. "I do know my products."

I waved an arm toward my house. "And I have this, the oldest house in the county. It's not all that great, I know, but it proves we were the first ones here. At some point, the Mayhews were first at something. And now they're just going to knock it down? Then what will I be?" I kicked at the step. "A nobody, that's who."

Benzer cleared his throat. "There's more to you than just a house."

"No, Benzini," Patty said. "She's right. You have to have something special about you if you want to survive Zollicoffer Junior High. It's clique central."

Franklin looked uncomfortable. "Actually, it would depend on where she moved."

I looked up, startled. "What do you mean?"

"We're assuming you'd stay in the same general area. But your father's business requires land, which could force him to move farther outside the city limits. Lou," he said, gulping, "you may not end up in the same school district."

Patty shrieked from the side yard, and I peered out my bedroom window as Franklin and Benzer chased her around the side of the house. I didn't remember how it started, but at some point on every bridge night, Patty's shoes ended up in the middle of the street. I stared at myself in the mirror above my dresser. I didn't look any different—same long blond ponytail, same three freckles across my nose. Except for the fact that my brown eyes were a little glassier than normal, nothing on the outside had changed. But I sure felt different on the inside. It hadn't even occurred to me that I might have to change schools. That knowledge sat like a giant bowling ball in my stomach. I smoothed down my new T-shirt. I'd left, saying it was too hot and I wanted to change, and they had pretended not to see my eyes watering. I opened the window and walked out onto the roof. One of the oak's thick limbs was just inches from the edge, and I shimmied across it to the trunk. From there it was easy enough to swing down, limb by limb, until I was on the ground.

I could still hear Patty yelling, and I figured I had another five minutes before they'd come roaring into the front yard again. Franklin's book lay where I'd kicked it earlier, and I moved forward to pick it up.

"*Boy Scout Merit Badges and Requirements*," I read. One of Franklin's top five long-term goals was to be an Eagle Scout before graduating high school.

"Looking awful glum for a girl at the beginning of her summer vacation," a voice called from across the yard.

I looked up to where Mrs. Hall, our librarian, stood. Since the library was right across the street from my house, I saw Mrs. Hall at least once a week.

I smiled weakly. "How are you?"

"Doing well, thank you." She walked across the street and stood next to me. "My diabetes is giving me fits, but I have only myself to blame." She leaned in and whispered, "I have a serious sweet tooth, you know."

"Well, sweets are good," I finally managed to answer.

"That they are." Mrs. Hall laughed, then looked over my shoulder at my house. "Oh, I just love this place. It helps me get through slow days at the library."

"Really?" I asked. I couldn't see how looking at my house could help.

"Of course. I can see it from my office window. I like to daydream about all the generations that lived here, what they were like, what they went through."

My shoulders slumped, and I could feel my eyes starting to tear up again. I leaned down and pretended to tie my shoe.

"Don't you wish these walls could talk?" Mrs. Hall asked. "Oh, the history they could tell us, the mysteries they could clear up. Can you imagine?"

"Yes, ma'am," I lied.

She stared at my face, quiet for a moment. "I don't know what's got you down, Louise, but whatever it is, my money's on you." She smiled. "You're a Mayhew, after all; your family tree has deep roots. Your ancestors were made of steel—don't forget that."

"I won't," I said.

"Well, I better get home before Howard starves to death. I've got a casserole to cook."

I watched her lumber slowly across the street and then went back to sit on the steps. If our walls could talk, they'd probably just yell, *Help us, we're going to be torn down!*

I thumbed through Franklin's book, checking to see if I'd damaged it. A paragraph caught my eye, and I read it again slowly. I read it a third time, making sure I'd read each word correctly, then jumped up and ran to the yard, where Franklin and Benzer were tossing Patty's sandals back and forth over her head. She was jumping up and down trying to grab them.

"Hey!" I yelled. "Hey! Stop it, you guys. I'm serious."

Franklin and Benzer fell onto the grass, each holding a shoe. Patty's bony arm whipped out and snatched them back.

I opened the book and pointed. "What does this mean?"

Franklin squinted in the twilight. "American Heritage. What about it?"

I stabbed the book with my finger. "Read the first two requirements!"

Franklin stood, and I handed him the book. He began to read aloud. "*Do two of the following: a) Explain what is meant by the National Register of Historic Places. Describe how a property becomes eligible for listing. b) Research an event of historical importance that took place in or near your area.*"

Benzer stood and held out a hand to help Patty. "So?"

"So?" Patty said. "It's boring as all get-out—right up Franklin's alley."

"C'mon," I said. I grabbed Franklin's elbow and pulled him to the porch. Benzer and Patty followed.

"Wait here."

I ran inside to the parlor and pulled the Bible from

the shelf. I quickly found the envelope, then raced back outside.

"Read this," I said, handing the letter to Franklin.

He read it out loud so Patty and Benzer could hear. "Interesting. Where did you get this?"

"I found it in the old Bible. So maybe something important happened here once. It says in the letter that the enemy was nearby."

Franklin shrugged. "I don't know, Lou. I'd have to do some research."

"What's the big deal?" Benzer asked. "Don't they just put a sign in your yard or something?"

"Yeah, but don't you remember the load of old doors Daddy sold last year?" I was getting excited. "The house we got them from had one of those signs, and Daddy said it was 'protected.' Even the homeowner couldn't make changes without approval from some history board. If we get one of those signs, the house is saved!"

"Wouldn't you know if something important happened here?" Patti asked. "It seems like something people would talk about."

"Maybe they do. Mrs. Hall said that if these walls could talk, they might clear up a lot of mystery. Maybe there was a battle here or something."

"Mrs. Hall?" Benzer asked. "When did you talk to her?"

"She came over while you guys were behind the house. What do you think, Franklin?"

"I don't know if being a historical property is enough to stop eminent domain, but it's worth a try. I'll look up Tennessee battles when I get home."

Mama's laughter drifted out the screen door.

I looked around. "Y'all don't say anything about this. Swear?"

"Who would I tell?" Franklin asked. "Tracy?"

"I won't," Benzer whispered.

Aunt Sophie and Mrs. Kimmel walked out on the porch.

"How'd you do?" I asked.

"The cards stunk," said Franklin's grandmother. She turned to look at him. "Are you two ready? I assume we're giving Benzer a ride home."

"If you don't mind, ma'am," Benzer said.

"C'mon, Patty," Aunt Sophie said. "We've got to get going too."

Franklin picked his book up off the porch and started after them. "I'll check into this, Lou. If it works, my troop would never get over it."

I waved at the car as they pulled away. "That's good," I whispered. "'Cause if it doesn't, neither will I."

CHAPTER 4

From the diary of Louise Duncan Mayhew
June 1861

*Walter has enlisted in the 2nd Tennessee Infantry,
and they have already been dispatched to Virginia!
Mother says our fate was sealed the moment Pres-
ident Lincoln called for troops. Imagine such a
thing—calling countrymen to fight countrymen. I
can scarce believe we are at war with one another.
Is this the right path? One day I think yes, and the
next no. I am in a constant state of confusion.*

Benzer and family drove up at 9:45 A.M., waited all of
about four seconds, and started honking.

"Lord, save us from Yankees," Bertie said. She sat at
the breakfast table drinking her coffee and complaining
of a headache.

"Bertie, you look like you've got one wheel down and

the axle's dragging. Too much fun at bridge last night?" Daddy asked.

"Tucker," Mama said, "don't tease. She's already in a bad enough mood."

I downed my orange juice. "Gotta go. See y'all after lunch. Bertie, will you feel like picking us up?"

She waved her hand in the air in a gesture I hoped meant yes.

Mama opened the lid of a pig cookie jar, causing it to oink, and counted out three dollars. "This is for the offering basket."

"Tell me again why you're going to church," Daddy said. He leaned back in his chair and held his mug out for more coffee.

I picked up the pot and poured him a new cup, stalling. I couldn't tell them about the Bible and Benzer's promise. They stared at me, waiting. "I don't know," I answered truthfully. "I can hear the church bells ringing every Sunday, and most everybody at my school goes, even Franklin and Patty. Why don't we?"

Daddy leaned over the table to pick up the creamer. "I reckon we've just never been churchgoing people. Not that we don't believe in God, but I have always figured he and I could hang together over a fishing hole as easy as we could in a church building."

I smiled at that idea. "I'll have to ask if that counts."

"So you're going to the Catholic church? That's a good hour away."

"No, it's too far. Benzer says they only go a few times a year. His parents are going to drop us off where Patty and Franklin go."

The Zertos honked again.

"Hush!" Bertie said, holding her head in her hands. "I swear if they don't stop, I'm going to tear the hood off of that car."

Mama squeezed me around the middle. "I think it's great that you're developing an interest in the spiritual. We could use some of that around here. Now, get going before Bertie comes completely unglued."

Mr. Zerto sat in the front, chewing on an unlit cigar, while Benzer's mom drank coffee and played with the radio.

"Hey," Benzer said. He looked half asleep and a little bit grumpy.

"Hey." I slid into the backseat. "Morning, Mr. Zerto. My grandmother said she'll pick us up and bring Benzer home so you don't have to make a second trip."

"That works," Mr. Zerto said. "Where exactly is this church?"

"Take Crocker Highway for four miles," his wife answered. "It's on the left." She turned to smile at me. "You look pretty, Lou. Is that a new dress?"

"No, ma'am," I answered, pulling self-consciously at the hem. I hadn't worn this dress since my cousin Stephanie's wedding two years ago. If there was any kneeling at this church, I'd probably moon half the congregation!

We'd picked a good Sunday to start going—it was Homecoming, a picnic held once a year. Tables were set up under the trees, and a couple of women were placing rocks on the edges of the tablecloths to keep them from blowing off in the wind.

Benzer and I weaved our way through the crowded parking lot. Tommy Winton, a fifth grader, took one look at me and dropped his Bible.

"Lou Mayhew, what are you doing here?" he screeched from across the parking lot.

"Getting a pedicure—what does it look like?"

He laughed. "Pedicure, that's funny. Hey, you want to sit with me after church? You and Benzer, I mean."

I grabbed Benzer's arm. "Sorry, we told his parents we'd sit with them."

Benzer led us up the stairs into the foyer. "Lou," he whispered, "you just told a lie at church."

"So? It's the perfect place—I can ask to be forgiven while I'm here. Besides, Tommy Winton drives me crazy."

I spotted Patty's red hair in the front row, next to Franklin. She was a good three inches taller than he was, and Franklin wasn't short. I motioned for her to scoot over, and we slid into the pew.

"Who drives you crazy?" Franklin asked.

I pointed across the aisle at Tommy Winton. He was craning his neck to peer at me, and when he noticed us looking, blushed a bright red.

"That's 'cause he loves you," Patty sang in a quiet voice. "Tom and Lou, sitting in a tree, *K-I-S-S*—oomph! Hey, that hurt!" She rubbed her ribs.

"Good. That's what I was going for."

Benzer grinned. "This church thing is really working out."

"I can't believe you actually came," Patty said. "That's some powerful Bible you have."

"So you still think it was the prayer?" I asked.

"Sure," Patty said, smacking her gum loudly. "Nothing exciting ever happens, then you guys pray, and—bam— the house is in trouble and you appear in church and Isaac gets cheated out of the scholarship. What else could it be?"

Franklin leaned in to whisper. "Obviously it could all be a coincidence. But the Bible is full of examples of answered prayer. You will find it difficult to prove either way."

"Thank you, Pastor Franklin," Patty said.

I looked around. "Could y'all sit further up front next time?" I asked, whispering. "Why didn't we just sit at the pulpit?"

Patty smirked. "Pastor Brian asked us to sit here; we help pass out the offering basket. If you don't like it, you can go sit in the back with Mama. But she would have shushed you three times by now."

I was thinking up a smart answer when the song leader asked us to stand. Everyone started singing "How Great Thou Art," but by the time I found it in the hymnal, they were on to another one. After a few more hymns and a prayer, we sat down.

The pastor wasn't what I'd expected. Most of the preachers I'd seen on TV wore suits and had slicked-back hair. Pastor Brian was wearing jeans, and his hair was over his collar.

"Welcome. Today we're celebrating Homecoming, and my first full year as your pastor. I'm glad that y'all decided to keep me." The congregation chuckled softly, and he began again. "I've asked some of our youth and high-school students to participate today during various parts of the service. We always ask children, starting from when they're little, 'what do you want to be when you grow up?' Then as they get older, it's 'where are you going to college?' and 'what's your major?' and 'what are you going to do after graduation?' It's like we're telling them that life actually starts sometime later. But I don't believe that's true. God can use them now, just as they are, and I want us to remember that as we continue to grow as a church body."

He told everyone to open their Bibles, and I leaned back against the pew, half listening. I'd never really thought much about God or that he had a particular purpose for me in mind. If anything, I'd pictured God as a giant fuddy-duddy who spent every waking moment figuring out how to keep people out of heaven. But the pastor actually made God seem kind of cool.

Afterward, everyone poured out onto the front lawn. The tables were now covered with fried chicken, ham, deviled eggs, potato salad, coleslaw, and Tommy Winton's mother's prize-winning apple pies.

Benzer and Franklin raced to the front of the line.

"Y'all better hurry," Benzer yelled. "The deviled eggs will be gone by the time you get up here."

We piled our plates so high they threatened to tumble over, and looked for a place to sit. Franklin's sister, Tracy, and a bunch of high-school students were taking up two entire picnic tables, while Aunt Sophie was chatting fast and furiously with a group of women near the drinks.

I spotted Mrs. Hall sitting alone on a quilt. I nudged Franklin with my elbow. "Mrs. Hall seemed to know a lot about my house," I whispered. "Maybe she can tell us about a battle or something."

"Y'all coming to sit with me?" Mrs. Hall asked, smiling. "I have plenty of room on my quilt."

We sat down, making a circle and placing our plates in the middle.

"You look a bit more chipper today than you did last night, Louise," Mrs. Hall said. "Things just look better in the daylight, I always say."

"Yes, ma'am." I took a sip of cola. "I was thinking

about what you said about my house. We were wondering if something happened there, like a battle maybe?"

"Battles? No, not that I'm aware of," Mrs. Hall said. "General Zollicoffer only passed through town. He didn't actually engage the enemy until Kentucky."

Franklin dropped his chicken bone on his plate. "Felix Zollicoffer, our town's namesake? We stayed in a house in Nashville once that was a hospital during the Civil War." He sat up straighter. "Maybe General Zollicoffer stayed at Lou's house?"

"Oh, I doubt that," Mrs. Hall answered. "He died early on, one of the first Confederate generals killed, they say, when his nearsightedness caused him to ride into a group of Union soldiers by mistake."

"And we're named after him? That figures," Patty said.

Mrs. Hall laughed. "I guess we could have been called Dibrell. That's the other general who fought nearby. Although I'm certain he wouldn't have stayed at Lou's, under the circumstances."

"Under what circumstances?" Benzer asked. "Was Lou's family against the war?"

"No, I believe her daddy's great-great-grandfather was actually a captain," she said. "I was thinking of the gold, of course."

"Gold!" blurted Benzer. "What gold?"

Mrs. Hall smiled. "Bless your heart, Benzer, your people

aren't from here, are they? It's probably just a rumor, anyway, right, Louise?"

I smiled weakly. I had no idea what she was talking about, but if my family hadn't mentioned it before now, it probably wasn't good.

"I'm speaking of the gold that was stolen," Mrs. Hall continued. "It was why General Dibrell was in town, you know, to replenish the coffers before engaging the enemy. He couldn't very well go stay at the Mayhew house after the incident."

Patty shook her head. "What incident, Mrs. Hall? What does gold have to do with Lou's house?"

"Well, dear, the story goes that the gold General Dibrell came to get was stolen. I'm sorry to say that the chief suspect was Walter Mayhew, Lou's great-great-great-grandfather."

I sulked most of the ride home. Bertie had driven into the parking lot, yelled at us to fix her a plate, then sat, radio blaring out the windows, until Benzer and I settled into the backseat. We hadn't had time to ask Mrs. Hall any more questions, not that I'd even have known where to start.

"The letter I found was signed WLM," I had whispered to Benzer as we walked to the car. "Walter Mayhew. The L must stand for loser."

"Maybe the gold was what he was saying to be cautious about," he whispered back.

If Bertie noticed I was quiet after dropping off Benzer, she didn't comment. Of all the things I'd expected to hear about my family, having a gold-stealing ancestor wasn't one of them. For twelve years, *twelve years*, my family had hidden this from me. They hardly told me anything—not about the past, not about the house, and certainly not about the future. It was so frustrating!

I stared out the window. What else weren't they telling me? Mr. Norman, our social studies teacher, had a phrase written on the board that he made us memorize: TRUST BUT VERIFY. He said that we should examine everything we heard, or else we'd be at the mercy of those who wrote the books. But what about what you didn't hear? You couldn't verify what you didn't know.

A small spiral notebook lay on the floorboard of the backseat. I picked it up and flipped through it; the pages were blank. "Hey, Bertie, can I have this?"

She looked up in the rearview mirror. "Sure, they were giving them away for free at the bank. There's probably a pen down there somewhere."

I dug around under the seat until I found it. In big, broad strokes, I wrote across the top, THE VERIFIED TRUTH ABOUT THE MAYHEWS. Mrs. Hall had said I had ancestors of steel, so I wrote that down. I chewed on the end of the pen. But ancestors of steel and gold thieves didn't go together. There had to be more to the story, and I was going to do everything I could to find out.

CHAPTER 5

From the diary of Louise Duncan Mayhew
July 1861

I received a letter from Walter that concerns me greatly.—"Dear Louise, I trust that you have heard of the battle at Manassas. Recalling it in detail is more than I care to bare, but I hardly see how it will ever be forgotten. I will not burden you with it, exsept to say that to call it a victory for the Rebels seems blasphemous. Jeb Bilbrey was killed and Tom Brian wounded. There were many more deaths, and while their names would mean nothing to you, they have made a lasting impression on me. This battle has affected me deeply, and I fear that if this conflict is not resolved soon, the man you agreed to marry will no longer exist."

Bertie had barely stopped the car before I jumped out. "I'm getting out of these clothes," I yelled over my shoulder.

Upstairs, I took off my dress and hung it back in the closet. I pulled on a faded pair of denim shorts and dug a dirty T-shirt out of the hamper. Some people like comfort foods; I like comfort clothes. I could already feel the anger from before being replaced with something more like sadness.

The wavy glass distorted the scene below, but I could see Daddy and Isaac piling up scraps of cast-off machinery. I rested my forehead against the glass pane and tried to imagine living somewhere else. I pictured Benzer's brick house with its two-car garage, and the rental cottage Patty had moved into after her parents' divorce, complete with its beige carpeting and white walls. No matter how hard I tried, I couldn't see myself in any of those rooms. Sure, our front porch sagged, but when the sun shone through the gingerbread trim, it made a cool pattern against the wall. And I loved that I could sit on our roof, the part above the porch, just by opening my bedroom window and stepping outside. Sitting on the shingles, under the shade of the big oak tree, and watching as teenagers drove up and down the street on their way to the ball field was one of my favorite pastimes. How could it all be torn down? My eyes filled with tears, and I wiped them away with my sleeve.

I looked down again and saw Isaac, sweat soaking through his T-shirt as he worked his shovel into the hard ground. Daddy was still going through the scrap metal pile, piece by piece, with a determined look on his face. He hadn't told me about the house, but I could see he was trying hard to get the twenty-five thousand dollars to save it. I let out a long breath, letting the last of the anger out with it.

I picked the notebook off the bed, where I'd tossed it, and hid it deep in my sock drawer. Tonight I'd write down everything I'd learned so far. Dad and Isaac weren't quitting, and neither was I. We'd find a way out of this mess. We just had to.

I walked through the junkyard's gate in time to see Isaac freeing a rusty piece of metal from the dirt. His Green Day T-shirt was stained, and his jeans were dirty, but I thought he looked like those models on posters at the mall. Coach Peeler might not like his skin color, but I sure did. It was way nicer than my pasty-white color. I waved, and he took off the headphones he was wearing and placed them around his neck.

"Hey! What are you doing working on a Sunday?" I asked.

Isaac leaned on the handle of his shovel. "Hi, Lou! Your daddy wants to organize the junkyard. We're going to take this load of scrap metal to Cookeville, and he's got some refrigerators to sell at the Crossville flea market. I'm happy to help, since I need all the money I can get."

"Daddy told me about the scholarship," I said. "That's just wrong."

"Thanks," Isaac said.

"I overheard some people at church complaining about

it. For a bunch of church folks, they were saying some ugly things."

"They were saying some pretty ugly things at my church too," Isaac said. "I guess I shouldn't have expected much from Coach Peeler, anyway."

"Can you do anything about it? I don't know, appeal it or something?"

"Nah, it doesn't work that way."

"But you've already been accepted at UT. You've got to go there—you're their biggest fan ever, next to me."

"Hey," he said, grabbing me in a hug. "Don't look like that, Lou. I've got a bunch of options. Please let me worry about it."

"Yeah, yeah, okay," I said. I pointed to the headphones. "What are you listening to?"

"I made a new heavy metal playlist." He grinned. "It goes with my moving-heavy-metal job."

"Sounds good, but I prefer *junk*-rock."

He groaned. "That was seriously awful."

"Seriously funny you mean." I looked around. "Need some help?"

"You want to help me dig the rest of these out?"

I nodded. It would take a whole lot of scrap metal and rusty rebar to raise twenty-five thousand dollars, but if they wanted to try, I was game. "I'm ready when you are."

Isaac handed me his headphones and MP3 player. "If

you're going to help, you'll need a little Metallica to get you going."

"Better or worse than Foo Fighters?"

"Totally different—heavy metal versus grunge rock. You'll see." He held out the shovel. "Start digging."

We'd just thrown the last piece of metal on the truck when I heard Mama's car in the driveway. A few minutes later, she came into the backyard carrying a bag with the words JACKSON ARTS AND CRAFTS printed across the front.

"Tucker, things look better already," she told my dad. "I'm impressed."

Daddy gave her a quick peck on the cheek. "Did you find what you needed?"

She rubbed her belly. "I think so. I'm going to get started before this one wakes up and starts moving around. It's hard to concentrate while you're being kicked."

"Don't overdo it, Lily."

She smiled. "I won't. How was church, Lou? No lightning or earthquakes, I hope."

"No, just singing and preaching. Oh, and it was Homecoming, so we got to eat."

Daddy winked. "And you didn't call me? I might have gone if I'd known that."

"I had to fight Benzer and Franklin for a deviled egg as it was."

"Ha." He hitched up his jeans. "I better get back to work."

Mama went down the path to the studio, while Daddy and Isaac started loading the back of the truck.

"Lou," Daddy called, "can you get my gloves off the coffee table?"

"Sure."

I stopped on the front porch and watched everyone go about their business. I was glad to see that so far my parents seemed okay. Bertie says stress over money is the biggest cause of divorce. Maybe that explained what happened to Patty's mama and daddy. After he lost his job, Uncle Henry started sleeping all day and going out at night. Aunt Sophie kicked him out of the house before you could say "boo." Now he's the manager of the movie theater over in Sparta, with a new wife and baby boy. But Patty and I get to see all the first-run movies for free, so that's something.

Daddy's work gloves were lying on the table on top of some magazines. I bent to pick them up, accidentally knocking one of the magazines to the floor. The bright red masthead caught my eye. *Middle Tennessee Farm and Land*. I slowly turned the pages. There were homes for sale in Grey County, where we lived, but even more in neighboring towns like Crossville and Cookeville. If Daddy was looking for places to live, he must not be sure that he could raise the money for the attorney fees.

None of the homes looked like ours. I folded the magazine up as small as I could, then walked with it to the kitchen. I stuffed it in the trash can, deep in the bottom, rearranging the garbage around it so that none of it was visible. We might have to move, but it wasn't going to be because I didn't do everything I could to stop it.

Benzer and I sat on my front steps waiting for Franklin.

"When did you say he'd be here?" Benzer asked for the third time.

"Any minute, I hope!" We were as eager as Franklin to get started on his American Heritage badge, and we'd made plans to go to the new Grey County Museum. I pulled my notebook out of my back pocket and reread the list I'd written last night. It was short.

The Verified Truth about the Mayhews

1. Ancestors of steel, according to Mrs. Hall.
2. Family has lived in the same house for 175 years.
3. Relatives sold off most everything at an auction.
4. WM may have been a thief.
5. WM wrote a letter to Louise telling her to be careful. (Maybe she was a thief too?)
6. The house will be demolished unless I figure out a way to stop it.

I stuffed it back in my jeans. Hopefully, we'd learn more at the museum.

Franklin, wearing his Boy Scout uniform and a camera over his shoulder, finally rode into the driveway and carefully parked his bike under the oak. "Are you two ready to depart?"

"You could just say, 'leave,' Franklin. What's with the uniform? I thought Scouts were over for the summer."

Franklin straightened his neckerchief. "Since it's Scout business, I wanted to look professional."

"Gotcha. Let's go."

We were going to see Bertie at the Grey Motel before heading to the museum. Her usual morning routine included holding court at their restaurant and catching up on the town gossip. If we played our cards right, we'd score another breakfast and a personal tour of the museum. Bertie can't resist showing it off.

"Lou," Franklin said, "I do have some information for you."

"What?"

"There was a vote last Friday. We were right. The county wants to build new offices on your property. They offered to buy it from your dad, but he said no. So they voted to condemn it." He frowned. "I'm sorry."

I looked back at our house as we walked. It looked sadder. "If we move, I'll just die," I said.

"You're not moving," Benzer said. "That would not be exciting—it would be tragic. We prayed for exciting, remember?"

I frowned. "Yeah, yeah, I remember."

"Well, technically speaking, exciting does mean to 'stir up emotion,' so loss of any kind could be labeled 'exciting.'"

"Franklin," I said, walking faster, "has anyone ever told you how annoying your brain can be?"

"Yes," he said, sighing. "Frequently."

"Hey, check it out." Benzer said. He pointed to where a red flyer hung on a telephone pole. "Zollicoffer Minority Scholarship Fund-Raiser. I bet this is for Isaac."

I looked down the sidewalk. Red flyers lined both sides of the street as far as I could see.

"That's great. Especially since the chances of winning the Pride of Zollicoffer scholarship are slim to none unless you're white, at least while Coach Peeler is in charge." I shook my head. "It's so unfair how people like Coach Peeler and Pete Winningham get to mess with people's futures."

"That's why being governor is on my list," Franklin said. "If you want to change things, you need to be a person of significance and take action."

I dropped my head. "We can't wait that long, Franklin. We have to figure something out now, significant or not, and take action."

The Grey Motel parking lot was full. The sleigh bells attached to the door announced our arrival, and we walked through the crowded room to the booth where Bertie sat.

"What are y'all doing here this early? Isn't summer vacation for sleeping till noon?"

I shrugged, and the three of us slid in around her.

Bertie moved her coffee and newspaper. "Robbie," she called to the waitress, "if those biscuits are hot, I'm sure these kids would like some with your famous chocolate gravy."

Franklin and Benzer grinned. Chocolate gravy was the diner's specialty.

A few minutes later, Robbie came back with a plate of steaming biscuits and a gravy boat. As we ate, Bertie turned to speak to a friend in the booth behind her. I watched, amazed. I'd heard her come up the stairs to bed about midnight, and she was gone by the time I got up at eight o'clock, yet no frown lines, no bags under the eyes, no crow's-feet, even when she laughed. I decided, right then and there, Botox was a miracle, and if I ever needed it, I would get it. Her hair was fluffed perfectly, and she was wearing pale slacks with a turquoise top and matching turquoise jewelry. I glanced under the table. Even her sandals had a large turquoise band across the toes. I looked down at my own jeans and T-shirt. If fashion sense is hereditary, Patty got my share.

"Of course it's ridiculous," Bertie was saying. "Most of the town knows Coach Peeler is the biggest donkey's behind this side of the Mason-Dixon Line." She turned around and caught me looking. "Why are you staring?"

I licked the last remaining bits of chocolate off of my fork. "'Cause you look really pretty," I said.

That brought a huge smile. "Aren't you sweet? Should I be humble and pretend I don't agree?"

I laughed. "That would be a first!"

Bertie laughed along with me and turned to the boys. "Are you enjoying that biscuit, Franklin?"

Franklin wiped his chin with a napkin. "Yes, ma'am. It's delicious."

"You let me know if you need another one," Bertie said, winking. "I never could resist a man in uniform."

I rolled my eyes. Bertie would flirt with a rock.

"So we were kind of bored and thinking about visiting that new museum you're so crazy about," I told her.

Bertie set her coffee cup down with a thud. "What? Miss I Hate History wants to go to the museum?"

I grinned. "Key word—*bored*."

"The museum, huh? Y'all angling for a personal tour?" she asked.

"Hey, that's a really great idea," Benzer said enthusiastically. I kicked him under the table; he didn't have to oversell it.

The sleigh bells rang behind me.

Bertie made a face at someone over my shoulder. "Oh, phooey," she muttered.

I turned around in the booth. A short, pudgy man

wearing a suit was smiling and shaking hands with folks at the counter.

"Would you be able to leave soon?" Franklin asked. "I need to be home by lunch."

"Fine by me; I just lost my appetite anyway. Y'all go to the car. I'll settle up and meet you there."

Benzer stood, but not before he managed to stuff a whole biscuit into his mouth, his cheeks blowing out like a chipmunk's. I punched him in the stomach, causing a chunk to shoot across the room.

"Disgusting," Franklin said.

We walked past the counter and around the group of men that were still standing there.

"You think those boys are going to be finished with the bridge by fall, Pete?"

"They better be," the man in the suit said. "That's when their pay stops."

"If they are," another man laughed, "it will be the first time the county's met a deadline that I've heard of."

"Things have changed since I became commissioner. You boys remember that when I'm up for reelection."

I glared at the back of his head. That had to be the sorry thief who was trying to take my house. I elbowed Benzer. "Is that Blake's dad?" I asked, whispering.

Benzer nodded.

Franklin opened the door. "I call the front seat!"

I gave one more hateful look at the back of Pete Winningham and ran outside.

The Grey County Museum was housed in what used to be a shirt factory. It had closed a while ago, and since no one seemed interested in buying the building, the town donated it to the historical society. Bertie is passionate about a lot of things, and history ranks right up there. She organized the town ladies, and they held raffles, spaghetti suppers, whatever they could think of to raise enough money for remodeling. Benzer and I went to the grand opening, but we didn't get to see much of it. We'd signed the guest book—Verbyl Belch and Anita Goodman—and Daddy had parked us at the entrance taking tickets.

I could see why she was so proud of it. The foyer was very fancy, with gleaming hardwood floors and a greeter wearing a green top embroidered with zm on the lapel. I recognized her as Thelma Johnson, Bertie's ex-neighbor.

"Morning, Alberta," she said with a sniff.

Bertie just nodded and herded us through. She and Thelma have been feuding ever since Thelma married Bertie's ex-husband. The only reason they can be in the same room together is because they each know how much it irritates the other.

Carrying a paper towel and a bottle of window cleaner, Thelma walked over to the front doors and began wiping the glass. "Suggested donation is three dollars," she called over her shoulder.

Bertie snorted. "I've got a suggestion for her—find some looser trousers. Hers are so tight, if she so much as toots, her shoes will blow off."

I grinned at Benzer and whispered, "Who knew history could be so fun?"

"Bertie makes everything fun," Benzer answered.

We walked from the foyer into a wide hallway. There were several people scattered around, going in and out of different rooms. "Is it always this busy?"

"Yes," Bertie answered. "Sometimes even more so. The museum's got people thinking about their own history and connection to the town. We get all kinds of folks coming in to do research on their family tree and that sort of thing."

"Can we do one for ours?" I asked.

Bertie opened her eyes wide. "This day is full of surprises. Of course we can."

A door to the left was open, and we could see shelves full of Ball jars. "What's in there?" Franklin asked.

"That's the gift shop," Bertie said. "We sell all kinds of good stuff; honey from the valley, homemade jellies, and local genealogy books."

"Are the Mayhews in them?" Franklin asked.

"Of course! It wouldn't be a book about Grey County if they weren't."

I started forward. "Let's get one now."

"Hold your horses. I've got lots of the same books at home on my bedside table."

We passed a room full of antique medical equipment and one set up like an old schoolroom. "That's a replica of the Maynard School," Bertie said. "I had to fight to get that included."

"What's the Maynard School?" Franklin asked.

"The school that used to be on Maynard Street—you know, where the black students had to go before integration."

I thought about Isaac and the red flyers we'd seen on our walk. "I guess things haven't changed as much as you would hope. You know, we're only two hours away from where the Ku Klux Klan was born."

Benzer ran his hand across one of the old wooden desks. "I can't believe it, but they're still around today. My dad and I watched a documentary on it. It's crazy how people are raising their kids to hate people."

"That's one of the reasons I was so gung ho on starting this museum," Bertie told us. "You'd be amazed how quickly people can forget their own history if you don't preserve it. And when you forget the past, you're bound to repeat the same old mistakes."

A man was staring at us from across the room, and I recognized him from the Tate Brothers auction.

"Bertie," I whispered, "who is that?"

She looked at where I was pointing. "You ought to know, he spoke at our Grand Opening. He's a prominent historian named George Neely."

"The opening was weeks ago. What's he doing still here?"

"Oh, he's doing some research," Bertie said. "It's very hush-hush. I suspect he doesn't want to tell 'cause he'd have everybody in town putting in their two cents."

We walked from room to room, passing displays of quilts, arrowheads, even a room set up like a 1950s kitchen. A large cabinet in the hallway held antique guns and swords. Benzer and Franklin stopped to read the sign.

"What does 'Rebel Relics' mean?" asked Benzer.

"Rebels was what the Yankee newspapers started calling folks fighting for the Confederacy," Bertie said. "Course, they didn't expect them to wear the label with pride, but they did."

"Because they were rebelling against what they thought of as a tyrannical government," Franklin said.

"If *tyrannical* means 'bossy,' then you're exactly right. That's why you find Southerners still using the term today. We're not big on having the government tell us what to do."

I thought about Pete Winningham. "I can see why."

"Of course, it would have been better if they weren't rebelling over slavery," Benzer said.

Bertie smiled. "So true. You got me on that, Benzer. But if the cause is right, being a rebel can be a good thing."

The last room we entered held hundreds of black-and-white photographs under a large piece of glass.

"What's this?" Benzer asked, leaning in close.

"This is a Who's Who of the town. It was a great idea—mine, of course. Everyone that donated money to the museum could place a picture of their most esteemed relation in here. Everyone wanted to be included. This room alone paid our expenses for six months."

The photos were labeled underneath. A sour-looking man in a black coat and high white collar caught my eye. "Silas A. Whittle," I read aloud. "Hey, that's the guy that owned our Bible!"

"That's him, all right. He was one of the first preachers in town," Bertie said, "and a close friend of the Mayhews."

I frowned at him. *And the owner of the magic Bible that brought trouble,* I could have added.

I walked along the wall, reading names. "Here's a Jackson and a Weldon—hey, Franklin, here's a Kimmel." I stared at the old photograph. There were four young people standing together. "Brody Kimmel, Louise Duncan, Olivia McDonald, and Walter Mayhew," I read. I elbowed Benzer. Walter Mayhew! "So Franklin's ancestor and mine were friends?"

"There are actually two Mayhews in that photo," Bertie said. "Louise Duncan married Walter a few years later."

"That's *the* Louise? The one I was named after?"

"The very one."

"Wow! And who's Olivia McDonald?" asked Benzer.

"A cousin on Louise's side, I believe."

"Bertie, how do you know so much about Daddy's side of the family?"

She shrugged. "I've always loved history, and the Mayhews are fascinating." She smiled. "Also I'm a bit of a snoop. Just because they're long dead doesn't make their lives any less interesting."

"Bertie," Thelma Johnson called from the doorway, "the museum in Sparta's on the phone. They say they never got the books you were supposed to send."

"Tell them to call the post office. I sent them a week ago."

"You tell them," Thelma said. "It's your doing, not mine."

"Mercy. That woman is as useless as a milk bucket under a bull!" Bertie followed Thelma out, stepping aside as George Neely walked into the room.

We smiled politely and then went back to looking at the pictures.

"Franklin, can you take a picture of them for me?"

He nodded and held out his camera. "I'll drop the film off at the drugstore later this week."

I leaned in for a better look at the photo of my ancestors. "Walter said Louise had a sweet smile in the letter I found, and she does have a nice one." Louise was standing in profile, smiling up at Brody Kimmel. "I think she's kinda pretty."

"Yes, she is. Brody is not bad, either. He sort of looks like my dad." Franklin took off his glasses and wiped them on his shirt.

Brody and Louise were the only ones smiling in the photo. Olivia was blurry, like she'd gotten impatient and moved. Walter looked like he'd swallowed a bug. "He looks too serious to be a gold thief," I said. "Did you find anything about it on the Internet?"

"No. The only thing that came up from a search of Mayhew and gold was a golf tournament in Mayhew, Mississippi. Gold sponsorships are one thousand dollars."

"It might just be a rumor, anyway," Benzer said. "Like Mrs. Hall said."

"Maybe," I said. "But remember, Daddy said no one would do business with them."

"That's right," a voice said from behind us.

We turned to see Mr. Neely peering over our shoulders.

He continued, "Emotions were high at the end of the war, a lot of families and friends never spoke again, but Mayhew had a particularly tough time of it."

"Because of the gold?" I asked, peering at the brown photograph. "Is that why everyone hated him?"

"Perhaps. Or it could have been the murder."

"Murder," I squealed. "Who did he kill?"

Mr. Neely looked at us, a surprised expression on his face. "You're related to Walter Mayhew, and you don't know the story?" He rubbed his chin, staring at the photograph. "It was never proven, of course, but some thought he killed that young man there, Brody Kimmel."

It was Franklin's turn to look stunned. "Lou's ancestor killed mine?"

"Yes, well, as I said, it was never proven," Mr. Neely said.

"This is just wonderful. Not only did my crazy ancestor supposedly steal some gold, but he was a murderer to boot. Why do people even like history?"

Mr. Neely smiled gently. "Don't take it so hard. Try to look at it as a puzzle. Your ancestors left you a great mystery to solve."

"That's what Mrs. Hall called it," I said. "What's the big question—whether the Mayhew dude was a run-of-the-mill murderer or a serial killer?"

"No." Mr. Neely laughed. "I was speaking of the gold. If he did steal it, he did a very good job of hiding it. It's been well over a hundred fifty years, and the stolen gold has never been found."

CHAPTER 6

From the diary of Louise Duncan Mayhew
August 1861

Cousin Olivia has arrived from Knoxville to help, since Mother's illness has left her confined to her bed and we are all stretched beyond our norm. I am especially glad to have someone my own age in the house. Olivia was firmly against secession, and is quite shocking in her statements regarding the ills of slavery. I trust seeing how much our lives depend on Jeremiah and Dode's help in the fields, and Molly, Lainey and Singer's for the housework and cooking will see her properly educated.

Franklin and Benzer talked excitedly the whole walk home, stopping every now and then to high-five each other on the sidewalk, and chanting, "Stolen gold, never found."

Benzer smiled at me. "Lou, this is awesome news. Why are you so quiet?"

"Oh, I don't know," I said. "Maybe because my great-great-grandfather killed Franklin's ancestor?"

Franklin took off his glasses and wiped the lens against his shirt. "Great-great-GREAT-grandfather," he corrected. "I admit that was an unfortunate piece of information. But I can hardly hold it against you, Lou."

"That's right," Benzer said. "And honestly—haven't you wanted to kill Franklin at least once or twice since you've known him?"

"Benzer!"

"Seriously, Lou," Franklin said. "Mr. Neely said people only *thought* Walter murdered him. It wasn't proven. It's not a big deal."

"Thanks, Franklin."

"But just in case, you don't have any weapons at your house, do you?"

"Ha, ha!" I rolled my eyes.

"Can we get back to what's really important?" Benzer said. "The lost gold?"

Franklin laughed. "It is a very exciting development. I think we should make plans on where to go from here."

"Isn't it pretty obvious?" Benzer asked. "I say we find it!"

"Well, I guess that would show Sally Martin!" I said. "You went on a cruise? Big whoop, we spent the summer figuring out a Civil War mystery and finding gold!"

Benzer punched me playfully on the shoulder. "See? I knew that Bible was the real deal."

"I wish we'd had more time to talk to Mr. Neely," Franklin said. "Between him and Mrs. Hall, we'd probably learn a lot about what to do next."

We crossed the street, jumped the ditch, and stood in front of my house.

"So what's first, Franklin?" Benzer asked. "The house or the yard?"

"I vote for the house," I said. "If it's buried in the junkyard, we'll never find it."

"Not without bulldozing the whole thing," Benzer said.

"Which the county is planning to do anyway," I added.

Franklin stared at us. "That brings up an interesting possibility."

"What?" I asked.

"There are other vacant lots within the city limits. What if Peter Winningham believes the rumors? That could be why he picked your land!"

"Seriously?" Benzer asked. "That seems like a lot of trouble for a rumor."

"They'd get the land either way. I bet Franklin's right. We have to find it first."

"Yeah," Benzer said. "Let's start with the house. Maybe Walter stuck it in the attic or something."

"I guess." I wasn't too hopeful. A lot of construction had been done to the house through the years. "But you'd think someone would have found it by now, and I'm pretty sure I've been in every hiding place in the house."

"But you weren't searching for anything before, and now we will be," Franklin said.

I looked over at the library. "Let's start tomorrow. First we should get some of the history books Mrs. Hall was talking about. Maybe there's a picture of what my house looked like before all of the additions. There's no use searching a part of the house that wasn't built yet."

Mama and Bertie spent the afternoon painting the baby's room a bright yellow. It had been a guest room before, and a perfectly acceptable shade of green. "Your father got that green paint from the nursing home," Mama said. "Babies need stimulating colors."

I offered to help, but Mama just laughed. "We still have paint on the ceiling from when you helped us paint the dining room." I acted insulted, but truthfully, I was glad to get out of the chore. I found a cola from Bertie's secret stash and went out to the junkyard, where Daddy's workshop stood. I wasn't getting a whole new room like the baby, but the box I'd found at the auction would look cool at the end of my bed.

The familiar smell of oil and sawdust hit me as I opened the door. Rows of assorted machinery lined the floor. A long workbench ran the length of the back wall, covered with tools, old paint cans full of nails, and scraps of wood.

The box was sitting on the counter next to a can of paint remover Daddy had left out. I smiled; he had already removed the hinges for me.

I opened the window and put on a paper mask. I found a brush, dipped it in the remover, and began covering the box. Even through the mask I could smell the fumes, but the paint began to melt and run off.

I took a wire brush and worked the remover into the grooves and around the carvings. They were very detailed. Little birds held branches with leaves and vines covered with fruit. On the back, in the middle where all the birds and fruit met, was an oak tree. The only flaw was a tiny wormhole near one of the leaves.

"You're still pretty," I said, admiring it. Daddy always said I got the love for making old things new from him.

After I locked up the shop, I sat down on a pile of roofing shingles and drained my cola.

Looking at the top part of my house that was visible over the fence, I tried to imagine what it used to look like. Could there really be gold hidden in there somewhere? The chances of it still being in the house were next to nothing, and if it was outside under the junk, we'd never find it.

Bertie and Mama had finished painting by the time I got back upstairs, but Bertie had left two pieces of paper on my bed. The sticky note in the corner read *Nice historians share their research*. For a minute, I thought she was talking about *my* research, but the papers were copies of genealogy charts, one for each side of the family.

I looked over Mama's side briefly, then put it away for later and stared at the one with MAYHEW written across the top. The lowest branch had my name on it. Above that was written *Tucker and Lily Mayhew*. Since Daddy didn't have any brothers or sisters, the line went straight up from his name to my grandparents', John Mayhew and Melissa Stansberry. I followed the lines up through two other generations until I found the name Walter Lowery Mayhew. It was crazy to think that these people once lived right here in this very house. Walter and Louise had walked these halls during the Civil War, the *Civil War*. I ran my finger across the word *Mayhew*. No matter what my relatives had or hadn't done, I was here because of them. If they hadn't lived, good, bad, or thieving, I wouldn't be here. It was almost too much to take in.

I pulled my notebook from my sock drawer and began to copy down the information. Mr. Neely had said to think of it like a puzzle. Maybe this was a piece that would help save my house—I mean, our house.

The plan to visit the library hit a snag before it even began. Franklin couldn't come; his bike chain had broken.

"Couldn't your sister give you a ride?" I'd asked him earlier when he'd called.

"No, she's at the lake with Drew Canton."

"She's dating him? Gross."

Franklin cleared his throat. "I have no control over what Tracy does. Although Drew is not the worst of her friends."

"How can you say that?" I asked. "He stole Isaac's scholarship."

"It wasn't his fault—and he doesn't appear to be too happy about the whole situation either. Tracy said someone used a key to write a very ugly word on the hood of his Jeep."

"I guess that's not surprising. Is your grandmother there?"

"Yes, but she's playing bridge on our computer," Franklin said. "I can't even get on it to look up battles in Tennessee."

"So you're not banking on us finding the gold?"

"Sure," he continued. "If Pete Winningham believes in it enough to steal your parents' land, it must be real. But the gold's been hidden almost a hundred fifty years. Getting registered as a historic landmark might be easier and would buy us more time to find it."

"Hey, that's true. And we wouldn't have to give the money to the lawyers. We could spend it ourselves!"

Patty had no interest in meeting us. Aunt Sophie works part-time at the antique store on the Square and could easily have brought her over, but Patty was having none of it.

"I'm giving myself a beauty day. I found a self-tanning lotion that all the Victoria's Secret models swear by." She yawned into the phone. "You and Benzer can handle it, but call me if you find out anything."

Benzer jumped the curb and rode onto the sidewalk in front of my house. I would never have admitted it to Bertie, but I had started to notice certain things about him, like how long his eyelashes were and how tan he was turning already. Oh, no. What if I became boy-crazy like Bertie? I threw a piece of ice at him.

"Ow!" he said, looking up. "What was that for?"

I put the empty glass on my windowsill, then climbed down the tree. "Being late."

Benzer parked his bike against the trunk. "It looks like the library is still there. So let's get going. I'm ready to find some gold!"

The air inside the library was as cold as the frozen food section of the Piggly Wiggly. After working in the sun all morning, it felt wonderful.

Mrs. Hall looked up as we entered, and smiled. "Are y'all getting a head start on your summer reading?"

"Not yet," I answered.

"We'd like to see some history books on Grey County if you have any," Benzer said.

"Of course we do. I'm glad to see you young people interested in history. Is this for a school project?"

"No, ma'am," I said. "We were just curious. Bertie took us on a tour of the museum, and it got us thinking."

"Thinking is always good. The reference section is against the back wall. Feel free to look through anything, and if you have any questions, I'd be happy to help."

"Thank you."

She winked. "Anything to help a fellow history buff."

The reference section was about fifteen feet long. Dusty, bland-colored books with titles like *Historical Atlas of the 20th Century* and *Tennessee Fraternal Organizations and Clubs, 1920–1964* filled the shelves. Benzer grabbed a couple of books from a small section labeled LOCAL HISTORY.

"Here's a good one," he said, handing me *Bridal Paths to Paved Highways: The Complete History of Grey County*.

"How can its history be complete? Is it over?"

"Just take it."

I carried it, along with *Pioneer Life and Living* and *Zollicoffer: The Early Years*, to a wooden table in the corner. Benzer followed, his arms full.

I was surprised to find the book I was reading interesting. "Hey, Benzini," I whispered, "did you know a tiger once escaped in town?"

"Wow. That's cool." He turned a page in his. "Check this out. A tornado came through and killed an entire family, all eight of them."

A black-and-white picture showed caskets lined up in a semicircle. "Ugh. That's awful."

We were the only three people in the library, and it was quiet except for the sound of us turning pages. Benzer closed his book with a sigh.

"Nothing?"

"Nope. There are a few pictures of town, but nothing before 1910. Couldn't you just ask your dad which rooms of the house were around during the Civil War and which ones are new?"

"That's not suspicious at all. Plus the house is just one place the gold could be. We need to see what the land around it looked like too."

"If everybody in town knows about the gold, why should you care if your parents know we're looking for it?"

"Hello? Haven't we established they don't tell me any-thing? They obviously don't want to talk about it, and I'm not really in the sharing mood right now."

"Okay. I'll ask Mrs. Hall if there's anything earlier."

A few minutes later, he came back and sat down. "The good news is there's a book called *History of Grey County in Photographs* that sounds just like what we're looking for. The bad news is it's out on loan."

"On loan? I didn't think anyone was allowed to take reference books out of the library."

He shrugged. "Usually, they're not. But for famous his-torians, they bend the rules."

"George Neely? That man keeps popping up every-where."

"There's another copy, but she said it's about ninety miles away, in the University of Tennessee's library."

"Darn it. We'll just have to keep looking. There must be something." I flipped through the pages in front of me.

"Hey, listen to this. *Bill of Sale for A Negro Man Slave. Hiram Eldridge to Lawson: Consideration—One Thousand Dollars. Know all men by these presents that I, Hiram Eldridge, for the consideration of $1,000, to me paid by Filmore Duncan, to have and to hold and bargained and conveyed, a Negro man to said Eldridge, by name Jeremiah, a slave for life.*"

Benzer frowned. "I don't understand how people did it. Do you?"

"No way."

I stared at the notice again. There was something familiar about it. I dug my notebook out of my back pocket and flipped through it. "Oh, no!"

"What?"

I slid the paper over for him to see where I'd copied down my family tree. "Filmore Duncan, that's Louise's father. Louise *Duncan* Mayhew. My great-something-grandfather on the Duncan side."

"What does this have to do with the gold?"

I threw the book on the table with a loud bang and shot Mrs. Hall an apologetic look over my shoulder.

"Nothing," I whispered. "But do you realize what this means? Not only am I descended from a murdering, gold-stealing thief, but now I find I'm descended from slave owners to boot!"

Benzer stared at the paper, shaking his head. "I can't believe it."

"That my family was so terrible?"

"No. That with all of that, Bertie makes fun of me for being a Yankee!"

CHAPTER 7

From the diary of Louise Duncan Mayhew
September 1861

The first battle in Tennessee has been fought in Travisville, just a day's ride from here. War and worry are our constant companions. There is little to console us, other than our faith in our Almighty. We are thankful for the Word, and for Reverend Whittle, who faithfully conveys it to us each Sunday.

The following week was one of the hottest in Tennessee history. The weatherman on WBIR kept going on about it, urging people to drink lots of water and to stay inside if possible.

We don't have air conditioning, so every window was plugged with a fan. It was like living inside a beehive, and everybody had taken to yelling to be heard.

"Lou, I'm going to the grocery!" yelled Bertie.

"Have fun!"

"We need buns?"

"Get some what?"

And on and on, we'd scream.

Since Mama was pregnant, she suffered the most and spent the days with a wet bandanna around her neck. When I offered to help clean the house, she said "yes!" with such happiness I almost felt guilty that I was just doing it to look for the gold.

Because I hadn't found any photos showing what my house looked like originally, and to make absolutely sure I wasn't missing anything, I cleaned everywhere. I was still angry about my ancestors owning slaves, and I took it out on the house, thumping walls and kicking loose floorboards as I searched.

"What's all that knocking?" Bertie yelled at one point. "It sounds like a flock of woodpeckers have gotten loose in the house!"

But no matter how dusty and dirty I got, or how sore my knees and knuckles were, there was no gold to be found.

I saved the room behind the bookshelves for last. I hadn't been inside it since the day Benzer and I had overheard my parents talking. I pulled the cord that turned on the overhead lightbulb and looked around. The walls were covered in knotty pine, and starting in one corner, I began to tap lightly on each plank. Benzer had said that

I'd hear a hollow sound if there were any hidden pockets behind the walls, but everything sounded the same to me. The only thing remotely interesting were some scratches in the far corner I hadn't noticed before. You had to be sitting to see it, but someone had carved a picture into the wooden shelf. I could just make out a beak, maybe a wing. It wasn't easy to see in the dim light, but it looked like a small bird.

The room was sweltering, so with another quick glance around, I turned off the light and went back into the parlor. A bead of sweat ran down my cheek, and I wiped it off with the bottom of my T-shirt. For just a second, I let the idea of moving settle over me, because the air conditioning alone might be worth it. It would be one less thing that Sally Martin could make fun of me about. I shook my head. If we moved, there'd be no Sally Martin. No Benzer or Franklin or Patty, for that matter. No way was I moving. The thought of me getting ready in some beige room with new carpeting, heading off to my new school, was enough to make me puke.

I walked to the window overlooking the front yard. I could see the library through the lace curtains. Mrs. Hall was right. Mayhews were made of steel. I gritted my teeth. By the end of summer, we'd have the gold or a shiny historic marker sign in my yard if it killed me!

That evening, Daddy announced that as a reward for all my hard work, we were going to the Dairy Barn for dinner.

Mama nudged me with her shoulder as she worked her way through an order of chili fries. "What were you doing over at the library again yesterday? That makes three times this week."

"Franklin is trying to get one of his Boy Scout badges. We're helping him research local history."

"Bertie mentioned your sudden interest in our family tree. Is that where this is coming from?"

"Yes," I answered. "But one of the books we need is still checked out."

As we were eating, Isaac and his girlfriend, Daniella, drove into the parking lot. We waved at them through the glass.

"I told you I own a whole slew of books about Zollicoffer, Louise. Why don't you just look on my nightstand?" Bertie asked.

I straightened. "I forgot. Do you happen to have one called *History of Grey County in Photographs*?"

Bertie shook her head. "No, but I'd like to. That's out of print and a collectible. One sold on eBay for over two hundred dollars."

"The library doesn't have it?" Mama asked.

I nodded. "That George Neely fellow has it."

"I'm sure he'll return the book in time for Franklin to get his badge," Mama said. "He's on staff at the Nashville Museum. He can't stay here forever."

"Well, I'll be glad when he's gone," Daddy said. "His

speech got people gossiping about this family all over again."

"As if people in this town need a reason. You know how much I hate being talked about. How many times have I said the best way to stay out of the news is to not make any?" Mama asked, looking pointedly at Bertie.

"It wasn't Neely's fault, Lily," Bertie said, wagging a French fry. "Not everybody's history is as interesting as the Mayhews'."

"Unfortunately," Mama said. "But it's not just the speech; it's the museum itself. The sad thing is that the Maynard School replica was supposed to remind us how bad things were," Mama said. "Emphasis on *were*. Now with Coach Peeler's shenanigans, it reminds people how bad things still are."

"If things are bad, we need reminding," Bertie said. "You can call a pickle a pie, but sooner or later, you're going to be bitterly disappointed."

"What was George Neely's speech about?" I asked.

"Something like 'Civil War Heroes and Zeros,'" said Bertie. "And your daddy is just mad that Neely brought the Mayhew name into it."

"He said something about the Mayhews? What?"

Bertie tossed her head. "Let's just say it was light on the heroes and heavy on the zeros."

"Can we give it a rest, please?" Mama said. "I don't care to revisit it, frankly."

This was the perfect opportunity for them to tell me about the stolen gold, but of course they didn't. I played with my straw, thinking. George Neely could be the key to this whole thing. He gave a speech, and suddenly the county wanted our land. Neely knew the history of the Mayhews, about the gold, everything. And he had the same book I needed.

Daddy stood. "Are y'all ready to go? I've got a few things to finish in the yard before it gets dark."

"I want to say hi to Isaac. I'll just be a second." I picked up my trash and walked to the front. Isaac and Daniella were leaning against the wall waiting on their order. Their backs were to me, and I was about to poke Isaac with my straw when I heard Daniella whisper, "If you mess with Coach Peeler, you'll be the one that gets in trouble."

I froze, straw in midair. Isaac leaned his head closer to Daniella, but I could still hear him.

"I don't care. You get that, right? He ruined my chance to go to UT, and you want me to just take it? I've been dreaming about going there and playing football since I was five years old." His hand curled into a fist. "I've worked my butt off getting the grades to get accepted. That scholarship should have been mine, and if I were white, I bet it would have been!"

Daniella shook her head. "What are you planning to do?"

I slowly pushed the trash lid open, hoping they wouldn't turn around and see me as I tried to hear Isaac's answer.

"Order two seventy-eight!"

"That's us," Isaac said as he checked his ticket.

"Lou," Bertie yelled from across the room, "are you going to stand there all day? Your mama's feet have swollen to the size of loaf bread. We've got to go!"

If Isaac answered Daniella about his plans, I wasn't going to hear it. Now I had another thing to worry about—Isaac getting into trouble.

I barely slept that night, kept up by dreams of Isaac chasing Coach Peeler around the Dairy Barn. At the first hint of daylight, I went to find Daddy. He was already in the junkyard office drinking coffee.

"Boy, you're up early this morning. You trying to finagle breakfast at the motel?"

I shook my head. "Not today." I sat in a chair and leaned my elbows on his desk. "I wanted to tell you about something. Last night I heard Isaac talking about getting even with Coach Peeler. You don't think he'd actually do anything to him, do you?"

"I sure hope not," Daddy answered. "But I can't say that I blame him for thinking about it."

"How can the coach treat kids this way and get away with it?" I asked.

"Racism can be very subtle sometimes, Lou. It's not always something you can put your finger on. It might mean being harder on the black players and more aggressive in helping the white ones get a place on a college team. It doesn't help that we don't have a large black population here. It makes it a lot harder to prove a pattern."

"But what if enough people think that Isaac should have won and complain?"

"Peeler's brother-in-law is the superintendent of schools, unfortunately," he said. "And unless you can prove without a shadow of doubt that he based his decision on race, there's not a lot we can do."

I groaned. "But what if Isaac does something bad? He sounded pretty mad."

Daddy set his mug on the desk. "I'll tell you what. Isaac is coming in late today, but as soon as he gets here, I'll talk to him. Okay?"

I nodded. "Why'd he take the morning off? I thought he needed all the hours he could get."

"He's spending the day in Cookeville. Tennessee Tech offered him a place on their team, so he's at least going to hear them out."

"But they're not even in the SEC! What would be the point?"

Daddy smiled. "It means he'd get to go to school for free—and play football. Not at the place he'd dreamed about, but it's still a good college. And he has some other schools that offered him scholarships that his father wants him to consider."

"Well, if so many schools want him, why didn't UT just give him a scholarship in the first place?"

Daddy took another sip of his coffee. "Isaac is very good, Lou, but you have to remember that Tennessee just won a national championship. They're recruiting the top players from all over the nation. And it depends a lot on what they need. Say they have twenty-five scholarships to offer. They might only have two for defensive ends. That's two open spots and a nation full of kids that want to go there."

"At least someone's organizing a fund-raiser. Maybe that will help Isaac get the tuition."

"Let's hope. That reminds me, I've got a lead on a scrap buyer in Knoxville, and Isaac is planning to try out for UT. If we can coordinate the two, I thought I'd drive him up. Do you want to tag along?"

"Heck, yeah! But I don't get it. If he doesn't have a scholarship, why is he trying out for the team?"

"I think he wants to see if he could actually make it. It might make him feel better about going somewhere else if he thought he wouldn't have made the squad anyway."

"Well, that won't work because he totally will! Oh, man, maybe they'll see how good he is and give him a scholarship anyway. Can Benzer come? And Franklin and Patty?"

"I don't know. I'm not sure I could keep up with the four of you."

"Then just Benzer? He'll pee his pants if he gets to see UT football players up close."

Daddy smiled. "Fine. You can ask Benzer. Speaking of Isaac, he found something interesting while he was digging in the yard."

Daddy reached into the desk drawer, and for a heart-stopping second, I thought he was going to hand me a piece of gold. Instead, he placed a small, pointy rock in my hand.

"What is it?"

"It's a Civil War slug. You said that Franklin was doing research about battles in the area, and I thought he'd like to see it."

"Awesome. I'll show it to him tomorrow at church."

Daddy closed the drawer. "I've been meaning to get out the metal detector. Maybe we'll find something else. I've heard Civil War buttons do pretty well on eBay."

I shot up. "We have a metal detector? Can I use it? I'd be really careful."

"Sure," he said, laughing. "You kids can have a little fun with it. It's in the shop. Remind me tomorrow, and I'll look for it."

I smiled. Wouldn't Daddy be surprised when instead of a few old buttons, we found gold!

CHAPTER 8

From the diary of Louise Duncan Mayhew
January 1862

We've just heard that General Zollicoffer has been killed at the Battle of Fishing Creek. It seems like yesterday that he was encamped nearby and the women in town were preparing meals for him and his men.

Church wasn't nearly as much fun the second go-around. First of all, there was the lack of food, but mainly I couldn't wait to get home and start looking for the gold.

"A real metal detector," Franklin said with a dreamy look on his face. "I've been wanting one since I was four!"

Patty snorted. "Are they all sold out at Nerds 'R' Us?"

If Pastor Brian noticed us fidgeting in the front row, he didn't let on. I was so busy thinking about the gold, I almost missed it when he mentioned Isaac's name. I looked up, startled, as Pastor Brian held up a red flyer.

"Some of you may have noticed these sprouting up around town," he said. "What you probably don't know is that I called Pastor Philip at Ebenezer Church and said we'd like to join them in their efforts."

Someone in the back grumbled. I turned around, but I couldn't tell who it was.

"Isaac Coleman doesn't go to this church, but he's part of our community. Now, I don't want to get into the decision regarding the Pride of Zollicoffer scholarship, but I'll say this. This church has a chance to show what we stand for, and the kind of attitudes we stand against." He laid the flyer down on the podium. "Faith without action is dead. We'll be taking up a special collection for the scholarship fund, and I'm praying y'all will join me."

I smiled at Benzer. I hadn't been all that excited when he promised we'd start going to church. I still wasn't sure if I believed all those stories about big fish and water-walking and other miracles, but if Pastor Brian was on Isaac's side, maybe he was right about those other things too. I'd keep an open mind just in case. I was still smiling as we were dismissed to leave.

Tracy Kimmel strode by with a terse "Franklin, let's go! Drew's coming over." She looked gorgeous, dressed all in pink, with her shiny blond hair swinging in a long ponytail.

"I'm going to Lou's house," Franklin said. "Grandmother said she'd pick me up later."

"Whatever." She walked toward her Jeep, hips swaying.

Benzer couldn't take his eyes off her and stared with his mouth partially open. The urge to smack him was overwhelming, so I did.

"What did I do?" Benzer asked, rubbing his arm.

"You look like a bulldog staring at a pork chop. She's dating the enemy, remember?"

Patty pointed to where Aunt Sophie was parked. "Y'all ready?" She climbed in beside her mother in the front seat, and I yelled, "Window!" That left Franklin and Benzer to fight over who had to sit in the middle. Franklin lost, of course, and Benzer and I spent the ride home pushing him back and forth between us while Patty giggled from the front seat.

We stormed, all together, through the front door and raced into the kitchen.

Mama turned from the stove. "What in the world? It sounded like a herd of elephants just came in the house."

Aunt Sophie's voice rang from the doorway. "They've been acting plumb silly the whole ride home."

"Daddy," I said, "where's our metal detector? Can we borrow it now?"

"Slow down, Lou," Daddy said. "Have a seat. Your mama and Bertie spent all day cooking for us."

I noticed the kitchen table for the first time. A sugar-cured ham sat in the middle, surrounded by antique bowls of fried okra, mashed potatoes, baby carrots, and turnip greens. There was a platter of sliced tomatoes next to a basket of hot yeast rolls.

"Yes, the metal detector sure can wait," Patty said, grabbing a chair. "What's the occasion?"

"No occasion," said Bertie. "Your aunt Lily is nesting." She pulled out the chairs on each side of her. "Benzer, you and Franklin sit next to me. I'm in need of some male companionship."

I sat down next to Patty, who'd already begun piling food on her plate. "I swear you have a tapeworm, Patty. You eat more than me, Benzer, and Franklin put together."

Ignoring me, she stuck out a thin arm and scooped more potatoes. "I have a high metabolism."

Bertie passed the food around the table. "Don't let her faze you, Patty. Being skinny and eating all you want is a gift of youth. Enjoy it while you can."

Mama placed a napkin in front of me. "Lou, have you been using the oak tree to climb down from your room again?"

"Maybe," I hedged. "Why?"

"I found more limbs in the yard. I said you'd probably been knocking them off as you climb, but your dad is worried it has a disease."

Bertie put some bread on her plate. "I can hear some of those big branches scraping right over my room. If they ever fall, I'm a goner."

"I'd never let that happen, Mother. You'd haunt me forever!" Mama said, smiling. "That's why we're having it looked at. Until then, don't be climbing on it, Lou. It's too dangerous."

"Okay." I took the basket of rolls from Bertie. "Daddy, what about the metal detector?"

Daddy was helping himself to a large piece of ham. "I'm sure it's out there somewhere. Along with the box you got at the Tate Brothers auction. You need to finish that so I can have my worktable back."

"Yes, sir," I answered.

Mama sat down with a loud sigh. Her hair had curled in the heat, and her face was flushed.

"Lily, this is the last big meal I want you to cook until the baby is here," Daddy said, pouring her a glass of iced tea.

"I'm fine, Tucker. It's just hotter than blue blazes in here!"

"I know you're fine, and we want to keep it that way." He turned to me. "Lou, I want you to start helping your mama in the kitchen. You're old enough to cook dinner every now and then."

"Oh, Lord," Bertie said, laughing. "Can I vote for takeout?"

"I'm for that," I agreed. "Being in a hot kitchen is not on my list of fun things to do."

Daddy gave me a hard stare. "I doubt it's on your mom's list either, but you sure are enjoying your food!"

I wiped a stream of ham juice from my chin. "Okay," I said reluctantly, "whatever you need, Mama."

"This is awesome, Mrs. Mayhew," Benzer said. He had a mound of greens on his plate, and Bertie passed him the hot sauce.

"Thank you, Benzer," Mama said. "Lou, how was church?"

"Great!" I answered.

"Well, that's enthusiastic," she said, laughing. "What was the message?"

"I don't remember that part, but Pastor Brian showed Isaac's flyer. The church is going to take up a special collection for the fund-raiser."

"I'm glad he could still find a flyer," Mama said.

"What do you mean?" I asked.

"Some jerk went through town ripping them down," Daddy told us. "All of the ones that used to be on Main Street are gone."

Aunt Sophie sat down and began making a plate. "Well, it didn't seem to hurt the turnout at Ebenezer Baptist this morning. When I passed by, their parking lot was overflowing. They were taking up their collection for Isaac today."

"That's right," Bertie said. "I hope they raised a fortune. That fool Coach Peeler has gotten folks riled up.

Did you see the letters to the editor in the newspaper? Roger Parrish said the scholarship debacle was just another example of how prejudice is alive and well. And Brooks Harris wrote something stupid in favor of Coach Peeler, basically proving Roger's point."

"Well, we've always had more than a few rednecks just waiting for a reason to fight," Daddy said.

"I hate that term," Bertie said, flinging her napkin on the table. "Why is it okay to disparage white Southerners but no one else?"

"No one else . . . how about Yankees," Benzer said under his breath.

I looked at him, sorry to see he was upset. No matter how long he's lived here, I can tell the Yankee stuff still rankles.

"Bertie," I said, "you talk about Yankees in a not-so-nice way all of the time. What's the difference?"

She dismissed me with a wave of her hand. "I'm just being funny. Besides, I don't mean Benzer."

"Well, how's he supposed to know that?"

Bertie rubbed her temple like she was getting a headache. "Fine, I'll try to think before I speak in mixed company from now on."

"See? It's such a minefield discussing serious issues," Aunt Sophie said. "Someone is always offended. I never know what I can say or can't say."

"But if you don't discuss it, how will you ever know?" I asked.

"That's right," Daddy said. "As a general rule, I try not to say anything hurtful about people, even jokingly."

"Speaking of things you can't say . . ." Mama passed the bowl of okra around the table. "Nelly Peek swears she heard Coach Peeler say the N-word at practice the other day."

The whole table gasped, except for Patty, who said, "What's the N-word?"

"You know, the 'N-word,'" Mama said, drawing quotation marks in the air. "The offensive word no one should say."

"You mean a cuss word?" Patty asked.

"Worse," Mama said.

"I thought cuss words were the worst things you could say."

"No," Franklin said. "This is way worse."

Patty's eyes bugged. "Worse than cussing? How is that even possible?"

I groaned. Patty liked to pretend she was so worldly, but she didn't have a clue.

"How is it possible that you've never heard of it?" Bertie asked.

Aunt Sophie shrugged. "It's not like we use it around the house."

Patty threw her hands in the air in exasperation, gold

bangles jiggling. "Can you just say it, so I'll know next time?"

"*No,*" everyone said at once.

Daddy frowned. "It's not a word you'd want to use. It's ugly, and hurtful, and brands the user right away as an idiot."

"Is it worse than saying the Lord's name in vain?" Patty asked. "That's one of the big ten!"

No one said anything right away. Finally, Bertie shrugged. "You'll have to take that up with God. I just know it's a word that has hurt a whole lot of people."

After we'd washed the dishes, wiped the counters, even thrown the dirty dish towels into the laundry, we were finally allowed to go outside. I removed the key from its hiding place and opened the door to the shop.

Benzer walked over to the worktable, where my box stood. "Hey, that looks better already."

"What is it?" Patty asked.

I shrugged. "Just an old box I got at the Wilson estate sale. I like the bird carvings." I looked around the dim shop. "Look in that pile of stuff by the table saw."

Benzer moved a tarnished chandelier to the side. "Is this it?" he asked. He was holding a long piece of equipment with a box at one end and a disc at the other.

"Yes," answered Franklin. "Flip the switch and see if it works."

Benzer found the black button and flipped it to the On position. Immediately, loud clacks came from the box. "Wow. I guess it does. C'mon!"

Patty and I stood outside the shop's entrance. "Where do you think we should start?" I asked.

Franklin looked around the yard. "Let's start with where Isaac found the bullet. Did your dad tell you where it was buried?"

"Near the side of the house. C'mon." I led them back through the fence to the side yard.

Franklin walked across the grass, waving the end of the detector back and forth. Nothing. He checked that the machine was still on.

"Maybe we should come up with a system, like mowing the yard. We'll start at one end and walk back and forth until the whole thing has been covered," I said.

"Sounds good," Benzer said. "How 'bout Franklin and I go in front, and if we hear anything, you two start digging? Hopefully between the four of us, we won't miss anything."

"Okay," I answered.

"Wait!" Patty yelled. "We forgot something." She ran back into the junkyard. After several minutes, she emerged carrying a shovel and an old bucket. "Now we're ready!"

A few hours later, we were tired and sweaty, all for nothing. We'd made a small pile of cola tabs, nails, and even what looked like a retainer under the oak tree, but nothing resembling gold.

"That stunk," Patty said, throwing herself down on the grass. "I don't even want to know whose retainer that was. Gross."

"Totally." I sat down and leaned against the tree trunk. "My aches have aches. I've spent the last week cleaning this monstrosity of a house, and now I'm pretty sure I have a splinter in my thumb."

Franklin leaned an elbow on the metal detector. "Operating the machine is much harder than it looks in the catalog, I have to admit."

Benzer sat down next to me. "So what's the next step?"

I shook my head. "Ask Franklin. I'm too hot and tired to think."

"I suppose the next logical step is to search the junk-yard," Franklin answered.

"Then the next logical step is to just give up," I said. "We'll never find it under all that crap."

Patty yawned. "I'm with Lou. There's fifty years' worth of metal back there. It'd be too deep for us to find, anyway."

"Hmm," Franklin said. "I hadn't thought of that."

"What now?" I asked, groaning.

"Well, the junkyard has only been here fifty years. Before that, I'm assuming it was just land, and probably the first place gold seekers would have looked. So there's no reason to look again. Either it wasn't buried there or someone found it long ago."

"Great," I said. "So some third cousin twice removed might have found it, and spent it all."

"Or maybe it never existed," Franklin said.

"Franklin!" Patty yelled.

"Sorry, I was just being honest."

"Well, stop it," Patty said.

I lay down in the grass and stared up at the oak, the one my mother had just informed me probably had a disease. This had to be the worst summer vacation ever. "Franklin's right," I said. "Let's face it. The gold might not even exist." I turned my head to look at my friends, my throat growing tight. "It's over, you guys. I give up."

"To be clear," Franklin said, "are you giving up on finding the gold, or saving the house too?"

"The whole shebang!" I yelled. "I'm officially giving up on summer."

CHAPTER 9

From the diary of Louise Duncan Mayhew
March 1862

A ruckus in town today provided excitement,
something most of us would gladly do without.
Mr. Altman gave a speech on the courthouse steps
that was pro-Union in nature. While I knew Olivia
to be in agreement, no one else supported his
position, at least publically, and he was driven out
of town by a small mob. Madness everywhere.

I was in a deep funk for three whole days until something
awesome happened. Posters showing a giant Ferris wheel
and a clown started appearing on telephone poles all over
town. The county fair is the best part of the summer, and
I'm usually so excited about going I mark the days off
on a calendar. This year, I'd been so busy thinking about
losing the house, I'd forgotten.

Mama teased me about going, saying we'd be out of

town or inventing some crazy statistic about kids falling off of Ferris wheels, but Friday evening, we all piled in the car. A couple of miles from the fairgrounds, we rolled to a stop. It's the only time of the year that Zollicoffer has a traffic jam, and we joined everyone from three counties on the two-lane blacktop. I could see my favorite ride, the Bullet, lit up and turning in the distance.

"Daddy, hurry. I want to ride everything before the little kids puke and ruin them all."

"Settle down. We'll be there in a minute."

"I told you we should have left an hour ago," Bertie mumbled under her breath.

Mama looked at us in her vanity mirror, but didn't respond. Bertie loves the fair as much as I do. She says she can get a whole month's worth of gossip in one good night on the midway.

Daddy handed a man from the Optimist Club five dollars and parked. I was out before the car had completely stopped.

"Louise Mayhew," Mama said, "you hang on one second."

I looked at my watch. "Mama, I was supposed to meet everybody fifteen minutes ago!"

"They'll wait." She held up a ten-dollar bill. "What are the rules?"

"No talking to strangers, no leaving the fairgrounds,

and no gorging myself on cotton candy." I grabbed the money, grinning.

"And stay together," she said.

"See y'all at ten o'clock," I called over my shoulder. I ran in and out of the parked cars, headed for the midway.

"Meet at the Ferris wheel," Daddy yelled, "and don't be late."

I rolled my eyes. We were late getting there; you'd think we could have stayed a little longer. I got to the Bullet just as Benzer, Franklin, and Patty were getting off the ride.

"It's about time," Benzer said. "Pete King almost lost his caramel apple."

"Yes," said Franklin. "You should have seen him. He was a very unnatural shade of green."

And Patty was a very unnatural shade of orange, I could have added.

"Been doubling up on the tanner?" I asked.

"Why? Does it look weird?"

I sniffed. A strange smell, like burnt rubber, hit my nose. "Um, no. You look great."

"Do you want to borrow it? All the girls in junior high will be coming back from summer break super tan."

I pretended not to hear her. "Why don't we go ride again?"

We rode four more times, and then everyone voted to take a break. Even Benzer looked a little sick.

"Would anyone like a burger?" Franklin asked. "My parents get home tomorrow, so we might as well spend the rest of the money they left me."

A few minutes later, we were eating at picnic tables, watching the waves of people pass by. Several kids from school stopped to talk to us, reminding me that the summer would eventually end. My stomach hurt just thinking about it. The only good thing was that I'd heard Sally Martin was still on her cruise, so I wouldn't have to see her.

"C'mon, you guys," Benzer said. "I think I can handle the Spinning Genie now."

"We'd better hurry," Franklin said. "The line will be extensive at this hour."

I swallowed hard, ignoring the knot in my stomach, and joined my friends.

We had ridden every ride at least three times, eaten caramel apples and cotton candy, watched the Fairest of the Fair contest—Tracy Kimmel won, big surprise—and lost all of our money helping Franklin try to win stuffed animals.

"You want to ride the Haunted Helicopter one last time?" Patty asked. "I've got a few tickets left." It was her favorite ride, mainly because the operator was our age and winked at her every time she handed over two tickets.

"No way," Benzer answered. "That ride is lame. Maybe the—" He stopped suddenly and peered over our shoulders.

We turned together, curious to see what had caught his attention. A crowd of people stood around the dunking booth. Coach Peeler sat on the small metal seat, his shirt soaked and clinging to his fat belly. I barely had time to notice the smug grin on his face before the *ting* of a ball hitting the target sounded, followed by a *whoosh*, *splash*, and he disappeared.

A few people in the crowd cheered, but most stood by, frowning.

"Hey, kid, give it a rest," shouted a burly man in the crowd. I recognized Mr. Kramer, the road commissioner. Bertie went on a couple of dates with him a year ago, but quit. "He's a drinker," she'd told us. "It's a wonder every yellow line in Zollicoffer's not crooked."

"That's Isaac," whispered Franklin.

"C'mon," Benzer said.

I had told the three of them about overhearing Isaac and Daniella, and we'd tried to guess what he was planning. Mostly we'd come up with egging the coach's house or something involving toilet paper. We hurried over to the crowd.

Sure enough, there was Isaac, standing at the booth. He wore Levi's and work boots, a white button-down shirt with the sleeves rolled back to show strong forearms, and a beat-up UT cap. My mind searched for a word to describe him. "Fierce," I finally said in a quiet voice.

TING, WHOOSH, SPLASH.

The crowd moved and murmured. "Stupid, uppity jerk. What's he trying to prove?" Their voices rang out clearly across the fairground, over the bells and whistles of the carnival games.

The four of us walked through the crowd, pushing our way to the front. Daniella put a hand on Isaac's elbow, but he shrugged it off.

I noticed Bertie standing nearby, and I made my way toward her.

"What's going on?" I asked.

She put an arm around my shoulders and leaned down. "Isaac is soaking the creep, that's what's going on. It's been going on for fifteen minutes."

"Three more," Isaac said in a tight voice.

"Just a lucky shot," Coach Peeler called out. "I've seen that arm in action. There's a reason you didn't play quarterback."

"Show him, Isaac," one voice called, then another said, "He ain't got what it takes," and "Somebody needs to teach him a lesson."

I wasn't sure if they meant Coach Peeler or Isaac.

The attendant pocketed Isaac's money and handed over three more balls.

"Drown the son of a gun," Bertie yelled.

I turned, scanning the faces of the crowd. I couldn't tell who was for Isaac and who was against, but the white faces outnumbered the black ones by a mile. One face stood out, pale and shaky: Drew Canton. He hung toward the back with Tracy Kimmel, peering around the person in front of him, as if trying to get a better view while staying unnoticed.

Isaac threw a ball. *TING, WHOOSH, SPLASH.* Coach Peeler went down. Isaac picked up another ball, tense, staring at the place where Coach Peeler had been, waiting for the next chance to soak him.

"We get it, boy," a guy called out. "You can throw a ball. Now, move on."

Daniella looked around, glaring. She looked like she was ready to march into the crowd and punch the guy. I moved forward to go and stand with them, but Bertie held me back.

"Oh, no you don't. Isaac can handle this without you."

Coach Peeler laughed, but he didn't look happy. He slowly climbed out of the water and sat on the seat. He'd barely settled when Isaac hurled another ball, dunking him again. He disappeared under the beige water, his Zollicoffer High hat floating along on the waves. He finally stood, waist deep in the water.

"That all you got?" he called.

"Get back in the chair!" Isaac roared.

Isaac pulled his arm back, ready to throw, when suddenly the ball was grabbed from his hand. He spun around, looking ready to fight, but it was Mr. Coleman, Isaac's daddy. He put his hand on Isaac's shoulder and spoke to him in a low voice. Isaac nodded, stiffly as if his neck hurt to move, while his dad continued talking.

The crowd stayed, watching, until finally Isaac smiled grimly and put his arm around Daniella, breaking the tension. The three of them walked, head high, off the midway without a backward glance.

"What, you done already?" Coach Peeler called to their backs. "I was just getting cooled off."

A few people laughed, already dispersing.

"Whew," said Patty. "I thought we were about to see a major fight!"

"I'm glad that's over," I said. I ran my hands through my hair, surprised to find them shaking.

"Did you see that ball?" Benzer asked. "It had to be going ninety miles an hour. I'd love to be that good."

"It's a good thing Isaac's daddy showed up," Patty said.

"Speaking of daddies," Bertie said, looking at me, "yours is going to whip us like a rented mule if we're not at that Ferris wheel in two minutes."

"May I have a ride home?" Franklin asked. "I don't want to wake my grandmother, and Tracy might not remember me for hours."

If ever, I thought. But I just nodded and started down the midway.

On the way home, Mama found a radio station and began singing. Her sculpture, *A Bird in the Hand*, had won second place in the three-dimensional art category. I didn't point out that there were only four entries, and two of those were from fifth graders.

We pulled up to Franklin's house, with its neat front porch and glossy black shutters. Even the landscaping was perfect, with a large water fountain in the middle of the yard. It was the opposite of my house, with its peeling paint and rickety handrails.

Franklin waved good-bye and turned to walk up the brick stairway. For some reason, watching him go into that dark house all alone made me sad.

I watched the countryside speed by the window as we drove home. There were no streetlights, and the inky-black sky was full of bright stars. I knew from science class that even though their light was just now reaching us, some of them were already dead. We just lived too far away to know any better. That had always bothered me. Maybe everything was just a glimmer of what used to be. What if my house, my old *life*, was already gone and I just didn't know it yet? I couldn't see anything to do but wait.

CHAPTER 10

From the diary of Louise Duncan Mayhew
April 1862

Father received news today of a horrifying nature.
A two day battle at Shiloh has resulted in thou-
sands dead. Cousin Olivia and I have spent the day
weeping as we are sure there are old friends on
both sides among them.

"**I** have a plan."

Franklin and Benzer were throwing pebbles at an empty coffee can behind the church. We had a fifteen-minute break between Sunday school and the sermon, so we'd headed to the shady area on the back side of the property. An old outhouse still stood at the edge of the dark woods, a creepy contrast to the pretty church. Most of the kids preferred to hang out near the parking lot, so we had the back to ourselves.

"Forget it," Patty said. She was perched on a cinder block, her scrawny knees touching, with a small pink Bible holding her skirt down. I tried not to look at her orange knees and ankles.

"You haven't even heard it!" exclaimed Franklin. He threw a handful of pebbles toward the can, missing with all but one.

"Whatever. I'm sure it involves me digging around the Mayhew yard, and I've had all of that I can stand."

Benzer kicked the coffee can, spilling pebbles. "What is it, Lou? They'll be calling us into church soon."

I scooted next to Patty, each of us with a small square of block to sit on. Mama had insisted on buying me two new dresses so I didn't have to worry about embarrassing myself. I tucked the hem between my knees.

"Okay, we have to find the gold, but we don't know where to look."

"Duh," Patty said. "Finding it would be a whole lot easier if we did."

I ignored her. "It came to me at the Dairy Barn. We've got to get the library book from George Neely. Think about it; he's everywhere we turn—at the Wilson auction and the museum—and he has the book we need. I went to ask Mrs. Hall when it was due back, and she said it was on loan 'indefinitely.' It must be important."

"Do you think he's after the gold too?" Benzer asked.

"He knows about it, so why wouldn't he look for it?"

"What do you suggest?" asked Franklin. "Following him around or something similar?"

"No, he'd notice us for sure, but we do need to get that book."

I picked up a stick and started drawing in the dust. "Bertie said he was staying at the Cornucopia Bed-and-Breakfast, right?"

Benzer and Franklin knelt down beside me. "Yeah, so?"

I drew an X on a square. "That's the B and B. On the right is the parking lot, and on the left . . ." I drew a big circle.

"That's the antique store," Benzer said.

"Right, and who works there part-time?"

Patty snapped her gum. "My mama. What does that have to do with anything?"

I smiled. "There's a side door leading out to the court-yard that the two businesses share. All we have to do is steal Aunt Sophie's keys and sneak into George Neely's room to get the book!"

There was a three-second pause, then they all burst into laughter.

"What?" I asked, miffed. "It could totally work. Daddy and I were up on the second floor of the inn last spring, picking up an old radiator. That's where the rooms are. All we have to do is climb up to the deck from the courtyard."

Franklin shook his head. "You want to break into George Neely's room and steal his book?"

"It's not his book, remember? It's the library's. And stealing is wrong. I just want to borrow it to make copies. Then we'll drop it into the library drop box."

"And how do you plan on getting into his room?" Franklin asked.

"That's where you come in. You already sound like you're forty years old; you'll use the store's phone to call the front desk and ask for George Neely. We'll be on the deck to see which room he comes out of. Nobody's going to lock the door just to run down to the front desk."

"Won't they just transfer the call to his room?" Patty asked.

I shook my head. "This is the Cornucopia, not a fancy hotel. They don't have phones in the rooms."

"So then we go in, grab the book, and shimmy back down to the courtyard?" Benzer asked.

"Pretty slick, huh?" I said.

They looked at each other, nobody speaking.

"C'mon, y'all. If we don't find that gold soon, someone will. Either George Neely or Pete Winningham—and I'll lose my house."

"But, Lou," Benzer said, "we don't even know that the book is important. It might not have any information that matters."

I frowned. "Then why is he keeping it? I've looked at every book the library has, and I've been through Bertie's stash twice. None of them mention a battle near my house or the gold. The book Neely's got might be a long shot, but it's our best chance."

Patty wrapped a curl around her finger. "What happened to giving up? I thought you were done with all of this."

"I know, but seeing Isaac the other night, and what he's going through"—I hesitated—"well, if he can keep fighting, so can I."

Patty nodded. "Okay, I'm in."

Benzer shrugged. "It's worth a shot."

I looked at Franklin. "C'mon, Franklin. We can't do it without you. You're the only one that can keep him talking on the phone while we search."

"I don't know, Lou. What if we're caught? What if I get kicked out of Boy Scouts? It could jeopardize the whole list!"

"For crying out loud, Franklin," Patty said. "I'm stealing my mama's keys, and Lou and Benzer are trespassing. You're just calling him. No one ever lost the governor's race from making a prank phone call!"

One of the teenagers came around the corner. "Church is starting. You guys better come in."

"Franklin?"

"All right. When?"

"This weekend, while everyone is playing bridge."

"Fine. But just so you know, my whole future depends on this!"

I sighed. "Mine too, Franklin. Mine too."

Once church was over, we spilled down the steps into the sunshine. Patty bounded over to her dad's truck. It was his weekend, and they were going to see a movie.

"Hey, Benzer. Are you riding with us?" Tracy Kimmel asked. She was leaning against the church railing, holding a Bible with a cover that said *Bible Babe*.

"Uh, no, not today. We have to give Lou a ride home."

Have to? Gee, sorry to be such a pain, I thought. I glared at them both, but neither one was looking at me.

"But thanks for asking, Tracy."

"No problem. Let's go, Franklin. I've got things to do." She turned on her gold high heel and stalked across the parking lot to her Jeep. Franklin waved as they pulled out onto the highway, barely missing Benzer's parents' car.

"Boy, is she . . ." Benzer's voice trailed off.

"A butt?" I offered, helpfully.

He laughed. "I was going to say hot."

"Explains why I feel like throwing up when she's around. Heat stroke!"

Bertie and my parents were standing in the front yard looking up at the oak tree when Benzer's parents dropped me off.

"Hey," I said. "What are y'all doing?"

Daddy put one hand on my shoulder and used the other to point upward. "Do you see that branch right about the porch line? Look at how the leaves are turning brown."

I nodded. "So?"

"So remember what I said about staying off of it until I can have someone check it out."

Mama put a hand on her back. "Oooh, I'm feeling this pregnancy today. Lou, come help me put lunch on the table."

"Sure thing."

"Why don't you just leave it, Lily? Lou and I will make everyone plates, and we can sit outside for a change," Bertie said.

"It's too hot for that. But I will lie down for a minute." Mama went into the parlor, and I followed Bertie into the kitchen to get the food together.

"Let's eat in the dining room; it's cooler."

I grabbed some napkins and silverware and made four places. Then I filled four glasses with ice and set a pitcher of tea in the middle of the table. "Ready!"

Bertie, still bursting to tell all the gossip she'd heard at the fair, talked nonstop for thirty minutes. When she finally slowed down to catch her breath, Daddy turned to me.

"A friend of mine is coming by tomorrow. Everyone else is busy, so I'll need you to stay home and show him around, okay?"

I narrowed my eyes. "What's he looking for?"

Daddy shot a quick glance at Mama. "He's an appraiser. It's no big deal, just a property tax issue he's helping me with."

"Really?" I said. "I'll be here. I wasn't planning on going anywhere."

I sipped my tea and listened as my parents talked. Other than looking tired, they seemed fine. I wondered how many lies they'd tell, how long they'd leave me in the dark before someone thought to tell me about it. I could feel the anger bubbling inside.

"Lou?"

Bertie was staring at me. "Yes?"

"I've been talking to you for five minutes. Have you heard a word I've said?"

I swallowed a bite of squash casserole. "Sorry, I was thinking about something else."

"Bertie asked if church was good today," Daddy said.

"Oh, yeah, not bad. Everybody was talking about Isaac and the fair, of course."

Bertie laughed. "He really gave Coach Peeler a soaking."

"Well, I think it was a mistake, and not like Isaac at all," Mama said.

"Lily," Daddy said, "Isaac's a good kid. He's just frustrated."

"I understand, but it didn't change anything. Coach Peeler is still dumb as a box of rocks. Only now people are starting to get ugly with Isaac—and with Drew Canton, and it wasn't his fault either." She paused to drain her glass. "Let's just hope the whole thing blows over."

"I hope it doesn't," Bertie said. "Coach Peeler needs to be dealt with."

"I'd be frustrated if I were Isaac too. How is anything going to change if he can't actually *do* anything?" I asked.

"You have a point," Mama said. "But honestly, things have come a long way. Tennessee colleges were segregated until the late fifties. I know you don't believe it, but there are worse things than not going to UT."

I dropped my fork on the plate with a clang. "And that's supposed to be comforting? This is all so wrong I can't even stand it."

Mama's shoulders drooped. "I'm sorry, Lou. You're right. Things are still bad for Isaac and a lot of folks."

I nodded, still thinking about the fair and how angry Isaac had been. I wished there was something we could do to change things.

"Daddy, do you believe in God?"

Mama laughed. "Boy. That's a change in subject."

Daddy leaned forward and rested his elbows on the table. "I'd say I believe the basics—God, do unto others. . . . What about you?"

"I think so. I mean, I want to believe in God, but I don't know how he could let so much bad stuff happen in the world."

"You're not alone. That's a question a lot of people struggle with."

"Pastor Brian always says God's for us and not against us."

"That's good to hear," said Bertie. "'Cause there's plenty that aren't."

I settled back against my chair. Pete Winningham sure wasn't for us. And maybe George Neely wasn't either. Maybe God would smite them or something. Now, that would be a good story.

CHAPTER 11

From the diary of Louise Duncan Mayhew
June 1862

Mother is ill with fever, and Father is often away
gathering news. Olivia and I are nearly faint with
exhaustion. Jeremiah is our rock, and without him
and the others, I fear we would be finished. I thank
the Lord daily for them.

A stranger was standing at the door. I held out my hand
as I'd practiced with Daddy.

"You must be Mr. Vinter. Daddy said for me to show
you around. I'm Lou." His huge hand swallowed mine.

"Nice to meet you, Lou. Is he here?"

"No, sir. He's out on a delivery." I stood back to let him
inside.

He seemed to hesitate. "Are you here by yourself?"

"Uh-huh. I mean, yes, sir. But I'm practically thirteen."

He slowly moved inside, pulling a notebook out of his

shirt pocket. "I see. Well, I won't be here long. I just need to take some quick notes and measurements."

I sat on the bottom step of the staircase. "Parlor's on your left, kitchen's straight back, all of the bedrooms are upstairs." I did my best to make sure my voice was steady. I knew why he was here. Franklin had explained that an appraisal would help keep the county from offering too little for our house!

The phone in the hallway started to ring. "Can I get that, or do you need me?"

"You go ahead. It won't take me long." He straightened his tie and started toward the kitchen.

I ran down the hallway and grabbed the phone. "Hello?"

"Louise! This is Thelma Johnson. Are you okay? I'm over at the library returning a book, and I thought I saw a large black man in your driveway."

I leaned against the wall, digging in my pockets for a stick of gum. "Mr. Vinter? He's a friend of Daddy's."

"Is he really a friend, or is he standing there making you say that?"

For crying out loud, I could not believe her. "He's really a friend."

"Well, I'll be watching," she said. "You just yell if you need me."

Yeah, right. Like I'd ever need her for anything. "I have to go now." I hung up as Mr. Vinter came back into the room.

"Did you say the living room was this way?"

"Yes. Can I get you a glass of water or some of Mama's cookies?" Daddy had told me three times to be polite.

"No, thank you. I had plenty at lunch."

I had started down the hallway when the phone rang again. "Hello?"

"Lou, what is going on over there?" It was Aunt Sophie.

"Nothing much, why?" I could see Mr. Vinter taking notes as he walked around the room.

"Thelma Johnson just called all worked up about something."

"Good golly! What is wrong with that woman?" I pulled the phone cord and walked as far down the hallway, and away from Mr. Vinter, as it would reach.

"He's doing some work for Daddy," I whispered.

"Why do you sound so garbled? Do you want me to come over?"

"*No!* I'm just chewing gum. It's fine, really."

"Are you scared? This scholarship thing has a lot of people riled. You should trust your inner gut, you know. If it's telling you something is wrong."

"Aunt Sophie! The only thing wrong," I hissed, "is with Thelma Johnson's brain. Call Daddy if you want. He'll explain." I hurried back down the hallway and gently hung up the phone.

"Everything all right?" Mr. Vinter asked.

I could feel my face turning pink. "Sure, no problem."

"Okay, then. Can I see the upstairs?"

He followed me up the landing. "There are two baths and four bedrooms on this floor." I opened the doors as we reached each one. "This is mine, Bertie is in what used to be a parlor across the hall, my parents are right here, and the one down at the end is the new nursery."

Mr. Vinter walked into each one, took a quick look around, made some notes, and came back out.

He pointed to a small staircase at the end of the hall. "Anything up there?"

"The attic. It's got a couple of small rooms in it. Daddy says they're bedrooms, but I can't think of why anyone would want to sleep up there—it's hotter than an oven."

He nodded. "Probably servants' quarters. This house is pretty typical for the time period."

"Then I was born too late. Having servants would be cool."

He wrote on his pad. "I guess I'll go outside now and look around."

I was still thinking about being waited on hand and foot by maids. "I can't believe anybody in this family was ever wealthy. I thought we lost everything after the war . . ." I trailed off. The bill of sale for "A Negro Man Slave" I had seen at the library suddenly floated into memory. Those rooms weren't where the servants slept. They were where the *slaves* slept.

I headed down the stairs, taking them two at a time.

"I mean, not that I would make servants sleep up there in the heat. That would be terrible. They could have my bedroom. I'd sleep up there. It's only fair, since they'd be doing all the hard work. And all."

Mr. Vinter smiled. "You want to show me the outside?"

"Yes, sir," I mumbled, and hurried to the back door. The slave bill of sale kept flashing before me, making me feel sick.

We walked across the yard, dodging the holes Patty and I had made when we'd used the metal detector. We went through the gate to the junkyard. "We're closed today, but normally Isaac or Daddy would be back here working." I looked at the piles of cast-off metal and tried to imagine it the way Mr. Vinter saw it. "So you know my dad from college?"

He looked around, making more notes in his pad. "Yes. We went to Tennessee Tech together. Met in art appreciation class." He laughed. "Of course, I was there for the art. He was there because of your mother."

"That's Mama's studio over there."

I watched him walking around, making notes, putting a price on all our stuff.

"It doesn't look like much," I offered, "but it has a bathroom in it. It's practically a whole 'nother house."

"Right. I was in it once, back when your dad and I were in college."

"You were?"

"Sure. My minor was in history. You don't see a lot of slave quarters in as good a shape as those."

I stood gaping at the building. Slave quarters? In our backyard! I wanted to cry.

"Well, I think I've got what I need," Mr. Vinter said. "Tell Tucker I'll call him in a few days."

I recovered enough to show him around the side of the house, past Mama's flower beds and the rusty birdbath she'd welded out of two broken wheelbarrows, into the front yard.

A police car drove by the house at a crawl. Thelma Johnson was peering out the library door. I glared at them both.

Mr. Vinter couldn't have missed what was happening, but other than a soft sigh, he didn't react. "Thank you, Lou. It was nice meeting you."

Stupid Thelma Johnson. I wanted to pick up a rock and throw it at her. "Nice meeting you too," I said. I held out my hand, and he shook it, smiling. Let Thelma Johnson chew on *that* awhile.

As he pulled out of the driveway, I stared at the library, where Thelma still stood.

"You can go in now, show's over!" I yelled across the street. "I made contact with a black man and survived— call the newspaper!" I marched up the steps and slammed my front door loudly. I hoped the old bag's teeth rattled out of her head! I snatched the phone off the hook. Benzer was never going to believe this.

After Mr. Vinter left, I felt sick to my stomach. I sat on the back stoop and stared at the roof of Mama's studio. It was one thing to say we had "servants' quarters." That made it sound like the people working here were maids or something, but the truth was they weren't. They were slaves. Real people, owned by my ancestors, had to work here and live out in that tiny building. Mrs. Hall said she wished walls could talk, but I was beginning to be glad they couldn't.

Daddy drove into the driveway and, a few minutes later, came walking around the back of the house.

"Where's your mama?"

"Still shopping with Bertie."

He sat down next to me. "What's going on?"

"Nothing," I lied. I stared down at my tennis shoes. I wasn't one to bawl, but suddenly it felt like I might start.

"C'mon," Dad said. "I can always tell when something's bothering you."

"Daddy, I can't believe our family used to own slaves."

I was beginning to think he wasn't going to answer, when he said softly, "Yeah, it's terrible. I remember finding out about it when I was about your age."

"How did you stand it? I don't want to even look at Mama's studio now that Mr. Vinter said it was slave quarters! Can't we get rid of it?"

"No, Lou. Those quarters were part of the original property, back when our family owned a large swath of town. When we sold the land, my grandfather had to take it apart, board by board, and rebuild it behind our house."

"But why would he do that?"

Daddy stared off into the distance. "I'll tell you what he told me: *It's important that we never forget our history and the awful things that man is capable of.*"

"Then why didn't you ever tell me?"

"It's complicated, Lou. Remember a few years ago when you did that Abraham Lincoln project for school and learned about how Tennessee allowed slavery? You were so upset. I sure didn't want to add to it by telling you about our own family's involvement."

"Daddy, that was years ago! There have been plenty of times since then you could have told me. It's my family. I should know the truth about it."

"You're right. But the truth isn't very pretty, is it?"

"No." I shivered in the heat. "And it makes me feel so bad. Like if Isaac knew, he wouldn't like us anymore."

"I get that—but Isaac knows that you have a heart as good as anybody's in this world. You should talk to him about it. I think you'll find that he wouldn't judge you for something your ancestors did."

At the mention of my ancestors, I made a decision. "Daddy, there's something else. I know about the county trying to take the house. I know we might lose it." I bit my lip to stop it from quivering. Even though I was about to cry, it felt good to finally spit it out.

"I'm sorry you had to find out, Lou. The last thing I want is for you to be worried about grown-up stuff at your age."

"Dad, I'm almost a teenager. I keep telling you I'm not a little kid." I picked up a pebble and threw it into the grass.

"I know you're not, but even teenagers shouldn't have to worry about losing their house. You ought to be thinking about boys, and your hair, and the latest fashions."

"You've just described Patty to a tee," I said, attempting a smile.

He put an arm around my shoulder and hugged me close. "Listen, I'm hopeful we'll come up with the money we need to fight this thing. I've got a couple of deals I'm working on, and the appraisal will probably buy us some time."

My eyes started to water again. "But what if we lose? The house has been in our family forever." I buried my head in his shirt, unable to hold the tears back any longer.

"Shh," he whispered into my hair. "It's going to be all right. Don't you know by now what's important? A house is just wood and nails, when you get down to it. It doesn't mean a thing without you and your mama."

I wiped my face with the back of my hand. "But I love living in town! I don't want to go to school somewhere else. I'd miss my friends."

He hugged me harder. "I know, Lou. Can we make a deal? I'll promise to do everything in my power to stop this if you'll promise not to worry too much about it."

I sniffed. "I'll try. But only if you also promise to start telling me what's going on. This is my life too. I deserve to know what's happening. I'm not Patty. I think about more than just fashion and boys."

"You're right. I haven't given you enough credit. I promise to do better from here on out, okay?" He stood up. "Now, you want to help me weigh some of the scrap I just picked up?"

I nodded and followed him across the yard. I may not have aged much in the last few minutes, but I sure felt a lot more grown up.

"Slave quarters?" Benzer asked. "And no one thought to mention it?"

I took a long sip of my milk shake. We were at the Dairy Barn celebrating his baseball team's victory. "Surprise!

This summer has been one big Whac-A-Mole game. Every time I poke my head up, I get hit with something new."

Patty placed her tray on the table and motioned for me to scoot over. "You know what really stinks? If you save the house, you at least get something out of all this. I just get the shame of having slave-owning relatives."

"C'mon, Patty. If you looked hard enough at any family, you'd probably find something bad," Benzer said.

"Yeah, but there's bad, and there's slave-owning bad," I said.

"I'm just saying the shame ought to be on the ones that actually did it." Benzer stole a French fry from Franklin's plate. "What do you think, Franklin?"

"Sorry." Franklin looked around. "I wasn't listening. I was thinking about the slave quarters and wondering if they'd help get Lou's house on the registry."

I sat up straighter. "Oh, yeah! What do you think?"

He shrugged. "It can't hurt. I'll put it on the application."

"But it's another place to search, right?" asked Patty. "Maybe the gold was hidden in there!"

"No," I said. "Daddy said the building was moved board by board. If the gold had been there, it would have been found by now."

Patty slumped down in her seat. "So back to square one."

I pulled my notebook out and put it on the table.

The Verified Truth about the Mayhews

1. Ancestors of steel, according to Mrs. Hall.
2. Family has lived in the same house for 175 years.
3. Relatives sold off most everything at an auction.
4. WM may have been a thief.
5. WM wrote a letter to Louise telling her to be careful. (Maybe <u>she</u> was a thief too?)
6. The house will be demolished unless I figure out a way to stop it.
7. Walter may have killed Brody Kimmel.
8. The gold has not been found.

"We've learned something new, so that's something. Franklin, can I borrow your pen?" I quickly wrote out number nine.

9. Mama's studio used to be slave quarters.

Benzer stared at the list. "I wonder why he told her to be careful. Be careful stealing the gold, hiding the gold, or what?"

I pulled my copy of the letter from the back of the notebook, along with the photo Franklin had taken that day at the museum. "It could mean anything or nothing. There was a war going on, remember? He could have meant *be careful and don't get shot crossing the street!*"

"The old-school version of Whac-A-Mole," Benzer said, laughing.

"Maybe we'll learn something useful when you get Neely's book," Franklin said. "Unless you've changed your mind?"

"No!" I answered. "This is too important. No one is changing their mind."

If any of them felt differently, they were too smart to say so.

CHAPTER 12

From the diary of Louise Duncan Mayhew
September 1862

Olivia and I went to nurse Dode today. He passed out while chopping wood a week ago and still hasn't recovered. Molly and Lainey have been busy preserving what few apples the Union left us, and I fear Jeremiah and Singer make for poor nursing aides. I'd never seen inside their home, and had Dode been well enough to forbid us entry, I'm sure he would have. What is propriety at this point when we are all striving to live another day? I was shocked to see they had but one chair between them.

⌒

Aunt Sophie burst through the front door waving a pair of bridge tallies like pom-poms.

"Yoohoo, girls, I feel a small slam coming on!"

Patty rolled her eyes behind her mother's back, and I

grinned. I was so excited I was practically vibrating. To-night was the night!

"Lou," Mama said, "I swear, you're about to climb the walls. What has gotten into you?"

"Nothing." I put my arm around Patty's shoulders. "Is there a law against being excited to see my friends?"

Bertie was looking particularly nice in tight red capris, heels, and a soft yellow blouse. A little nicer than usual for bridge night, but still well within her fashion range.

"You look awfully fancy. Is tonight a special occasion?" I asked.

"I'm meeting someone for coffee later."

I stared. "I thought y'all were playing bridge a night early because you had a date tomorrow night."

Bertie grinned. "Is there a law against having two?"

"If there was, you'd be a felon by now."

"Ha. You've got that right." Car doors slammed outside. "Dot's here," Bertie said, standing. "Let's get this show on the road."

We went outside to meet the boys and Mrs. Kimmel.

"Franklin, what is that under your arm?" Mama asked.

"It's a telescope, ma'am."

"Yeah, Mama, there's supposed to be this amazing meteor shower tonight."

"Meteor shower?" Aunt Sophie asked.

"Yes!" I answered. "We were thinking about walking

up Henson Hill watching for it. Would that be okay?" I asked.

Patty jumped in. "It's supposed to be awesome. They're supposed to be really close, closer than they've been in years, like, probably closer than they'll ever be—"

"We get the picture, Patty," her mother said. "What time is this shower supposed to take place?"

"The paper said about nine o'clock," offered Franklin. "The hill behind town would give us an unobstructed view." He smiled, obviously proud for remembering the script.

"Lillian," Bertie yelled, "the cards are dealt. C'mon!"

"Well, Lily, what do you think?" asked Aunt Sophie.

"I guess it will be all right," my mother answered. "But stay on the sidewalk, and if you're not home by ten, we're sending out the National Guard."

Patty saluted, and laughing, the four of us piled onto the front yard to wait for dark.

Huddled together under the giant oak, we went over the plan again.

"Okay, so we walk uptown to the antique store. You've got the key, right, Patty?"

"Right," Patty said, pulling a silver chain from underneath her T-shirt. She dangled the key in the air proudly. "Mama never saw a thing."

"Great," I said. "You're a regular Houdini. Now, once we're in the store, we go to the side door that leads to the courtyard."

"After first looking out the window to make sure no one from the inn is out there," Franklin added.

"Right," Benzer said. "Then, we go through the court-yard, and I'll climb the latticework up to the second-floor patio."

"That's where I come in." Franklin cleared his throat and straightened up to his full five foot three inches. "With my deepest voice, I call the desk and ask for George Neely. Benzer watches to see what room he comes out of, then while Mr. Neely is downstairs talking to me, he slips into the room, grabs the book, and scoots back down the lattice."

"Piece of cake," Patty said, "but I still don't know why we have to stay outside doing nothing."

"We're not doing nothing. We've got to help Benzer back down the lattice and keep watch in case anybody comes out there."

Patty pursed her lips and blew a curl off her forehead. "Why anybody would be outside in this heat is beyond me." She raised one skinny arm and gave her armpit a sniff. "I'm about to become offensive."

"Yes," chimed Franklin, "about four years ago."

I leaned against the oak, comforted by its familiar trunk, and listened to the sound of them fighting. The four of us together—that was how we'd spent bridge nights for as long as I could remember, and I loved it.

How would we hang out together if I lived in another county? My house wasn't the only thing at stake if we failed!

Taking care to walk the back streets, the four of us made our way to town. I felt excited and nervous and like I was about to come apart into a million pieces.

When we got to the back parking lot of the antique store, Patty took a deep breath. "Y'all ready?"

We nodded, looking over our shoulders.

"Here goes." She leaned her neck down level with the doorknob, inserted the brass key, and turned the knob. The click was unmistakable.

"C'mon, we're in."

"Hurry," Franklin said as we scrambled in. "Where's the phone?"

Patty pointed to the wall. "It's next to the door, so you should be able to see us easy enough."

I crept across the store to the opposite wall. "The door's right here. Benzer, pull the bolt."

"Wait!" yelled Franklin, causing us to jump. "You forgot to look out the window."

"Dude," Benzer said, placing a hand over his chest. "You about gave me a heart attack."

"Sorry."

I stood on tiptoe and peered over the windowsill into the courtyard beyond. A couple of wrought-iron tables and chairs were scattered about, but no people.

"It's clear. Let's get this over with."

Benzer and Franklin tugged on the dead bolt, and the door opened with a loud creak. Hugging close to the wall, we snuck across the empty courtyard, over to the lattice attached to the siding. Greenery grew up it in a thick mass, hiding most of the wood.

"I hope this isn't poison ivy," Benzer said, moving the plant to one side and finding a place to hold. He put one foot on a horizontal section, pulled himself up, and balanced there for a brief second, before the piece broke under his foot.

"What the—?" Benzer blurted out, falling against Patty.

"Oww," Patty whispered, rubbing her shoulder.

"Sorry." Benzer pulled the ivy leaves apart. "Man, half of these cross sections are rotten."

I pointed toward the back. "Try it over there."

He put his weight on another crosspiece and crashed back.

"Now what are we going to do?" Patty moaned.

I stared up at the balcony. It looked about the same height as my upstairs window at home.

"I can do it," I said.

"What?" Benzer asked. "Come on, Lou, I know this

means a lot to you, but that's dangerous. You could seriously hurt yourself."

I shook my head. "I'm not going to get hurt. I've climbed up and down our old oak a thousand times. Look, it's the only way. I'm the lightest one here, not counting Franklin, and we need him to make the phone call."

"What about me?" Patty asked. "You're no skinnier than I am."

"You're wearing platform sandals! They'll never fit between the lattice, and my shoes won't fit you."

A door closed somewhere above us, and we grew still, listening. The hum of Friday-night traffic was the only sound.

I put a foot on the first horizontal piece I could find. Gingerly, I grabbed another cross section and climbed up. Nothing happened. "See, it'll hold me. You guys keep watch when Franklin goes in to make his call."

Benzer just stared at me, shaking his head.

"Please," I begged.

"Fine," Benzer said finally. "But if you crack your skull, you can tell your mama what happened."

"Deal," I said, already climbing.

I made it to the balcony without any trouble and pulled myself over the railing. A sliding glass door led into the inn's second-floor hallway. I peered through the vertical blinds, satisfied that it seemed deserted. I gave it a tug, and it opened easily.

Stepping back to the railing, I looked down to see the three of them reflected clearly in the moonlight. I gave them the thumbs-up signal. Franklin gave me the signal back and ran over to the store.

I hunkered down, looking through the glass, while he made the call. A few minutes later, Mr. Kirby, the inn's owner, came up the stairs at the end of the hallway. He walked straight down the hall toward the balcony. For a terrifying second, I thought he was going to see me, but at the last moment, he stopped. He knocked on a door to my left. A sign over the door read MAGNOLIA BLOSSOM, #3.

"Mr. Neely?"

A couple of heartbeats later, the door opened a crack.

"Yes, Mr. Kirby? Is everything all right?"

"Yes, yes. I'm sorry to disturb you, but there's a phone call for you downstairs."

The door opened wider, and George Neely stepped into the hall dressed in striped pajamas and a robe. He wore a pair of glasses perched on his gray head and the aggravated look of someone who had just been interrupted.

He put a hand over his mouth and coughed slightly. "Did you get a name?"

Mr. Kirby shook his head. "I'm afraid not. Would you like me to have him call back in the morning?"

"No, that's fine. I'll take it. Probably someone from the university, research-related—that sort of thing."

I watched them disappear down the stairs, then I

slipped quietly into the hallway. Just as we'd hoped, Mr. Neely had left his door unlocked while he went to take his phone call. I checked my watch again. Franklin had a list of questions and hoped to keep him talking for at least five minutes.

"Please let this work," I whispered, and walked into Mr. Neely's room.

The room was small, and the wallpaper featured giant burgundy magnolias. A large four-poster bed took up most of the space. A velvet chair was sitting at an antique desk. Papers and books were strewn on top of the desk. I was so nervous I thought I might pass out on the Oriental rug.

I sorted through the books quickly. They were all related to local history in some way, but the *History of Grey County in Photographs* wasn't among them. Frantic, I began opening drawers and shuffling papers and stuff around. Just as I was about to give up, I found it on the floor, leaning against the desk. Grabbing it, I tried stuffing it into the waistband of my shorts. It was wider than I was, and I ended up turning it sideways and stuffing a corner in my waistband. My T-shirt stretched tight across the book, making me look like I'd swallowed a pizza— box and all.

The desk was a mess from where I had shuffled papers. I looked at my watch. Four minutes since I'd walked in. Quickly, I began to put the papers and books back as best I could remember.

I moved a stack of notebooks, and a piece of paper fluttered to the floor. I picked it up and the name Mayhew caught my eye. It was a copy of a receipt, dated 1932. I read down the list of items, mesmerized. Furniture, books, candlesticks, horses, wagons . . . the list went on and on. Scribbled in the margin were the words *Mayhew auction inventory*. I was still holding it when I heard a cough from outside the door.

Panicked, I looked around for a place to hide. Dropping to my knees, I scrambled for the bed. I'd just gotten underneath when the door opened. I lay still, my heart racing. The door closed softly, and I could hear low mutterings: "Silly questions, never even heard of the Nashville Historic Activist Committee."

I raised my head an inch and peered through the lace bed skirt. Right at the pajama-clad legs of George Neely.

CHAPTER 13

From the diary of Louise Duncan Mayhew
December 1862

We are cold. For days, the enemy has camped
in town, and we are trapped in our own homes.
They have seized all the wood for themselves,
leaving us to burn corn husks and twigs.

This was the type of thing grown-ups always said would
be funny years later. Like that was supposed to make you
feel better—that one day, when you were a hundred years
old, you'd be able to look back and laugh. But right then,
hiding under George Neely's bed, I felt like the world was
coming to an end.

My options buzzed through my brain like a mosquito
trying to find a warm place to land. One, I could stay hidden until he went to sleep and then try to sneak out without waking him. Of course, in less than an hour, it would
be ten o'clock. At that point, Mama would start looking

for me; if I wasn't on our doorstep, I might as well stay where I was—life would not be worth living.

Secondly, I could make a run for it—scramble out from under the bed, throw open the door, and sprint for the exit.

I chanced another look at where Mr. Neely had planted himself. I could hear him shuffling papers at the desk and see his legs. He was sitting right between me and the door.

"Honestly, I do believe I'm losing my mind," he said. "I know I just had the blasted thing." He walked back and forth in front of the desk.

I lay there holding my breath. In my hurry to hide, the book had fallen out of my shorts, and now a corner of it peeked out from beneath the bed. That corner was clearly visible in the room. If he looked under the bed, I was done for.

He coughed again, and I could see his rubber-soled house shoes pacing back and forth. Suddenly, he crouched down on the carpet, one knee just a few inches from my face. He put a hand on the bed skirt, and I was about to burst into tears, when frantic knocking sounded on the door.

"What in the world?" he asked, and raised himself with a huff.

The knocking continued—*rat-a-tat-tat*—hard and fast. A loud wailing was coming from the other side.

"Please, Sister, please, open the door."

It was Patty's voice, yelling like there was no tomorrow.

Mr. Neely slid back the bolt, and Patty burst into the room. I could see her shoes flying across the carpet.

"Where is she?" she cried. "Where's my sister?"

I could only imagine Mr. Neely was as flabbergasted as I was, for all he did was stammer, "Wh-who, who? Young lady, please calm down!"

"I'm looking for my sister," Patty continued. "Daddy found a note saying she was going to a party here tonight to meet a boy! Please help me, mister. Daddy's gonna kill the both of them, for sure!" Patty began crying even louder.

I lay under the bed and tried to understand what she was doing. I wasn't sure how this was going to help me get out of his room without us getting caught, but it was an exciting effort. Patty sounded really freaked out.

"I assure you, young lady, your sister is not here in my bathroom or closet, and you can see there's no party. I must insist that you leave immediately."

Patty's skinny knees dropped to the carpet, and she raised the bed skirt. Her eyes widened for a moment as they met mine, then she was gone again.

"Okay, mister, if you say so," Patty said, sighing. "But when my daddy turns up, you might want to talk to him a little nicer. He chased her last boyfriend off with a base-ball bat, and you don't look like you can run very fast."

I put a hand over my mouth. As nervous as I was, a giggle was fighting hard to escape my lips.

"Now, just hold on a second. What makes you so sure he's coming here?"

I could hear the smile in Patty's voice. "Oh, well, he told Mama to go ahead and get the bail money ready 'cause he was gonna burst into room number three 'fists flying.' Daddy's kinda protective of his girls."

"Good God. What kind of town is this? We're going to have to get the police."

"No!" Patty screamed. "You can't. If the police show up, there will be big trouble. Daddy's already on probation."

"I'm sorry, I'd like to help, but it's highly inappropriate for you to even be in this room, and I refuse to wait here and be chased by a crazed father." He strode to the door and opened it. "You're going to have to come downstairs with me and get this straightened out."

"Fine," Patty said, "but you'd better let me walk in front, in case we meet Daddy coming up the stairs."

I heard the door close behind them, and I scrambled out from under the bed. I waited for what I hoped was enough time for them to turn the corner, then flew into the hallway. I opened the sliding door and raced onto the balcony, immediately colliding into a body.

"Aiiee!" I screamed.

"Shh, Lou, calm down, it's me." Benzer put a finger on his lips.

"How'd you guys get up here?" I whispered.

"By risking our lives. We stacked a chair on top of two

tables and prayed from there. I almost fell three times."
He looked pale in the moonlight. "Let's go."

We jumped over the railing, grabbing onto trellis, vine,
whatever we could find, and half climbed, half fell to the
bottom, where Franklin was waiting. He grabbed my
hand and pulled me, running through the dark, to the antique shop's door. I flung it open, then waited until they
were inside to slam it shut. We raced down the aisles of
the shop. Benzer missed a shelf full of Depression glass
by a hair, but we made it to the exit without incident.
We stood on the gravel, breathing heavily, listening for
the sound of Mr. Neely or Mr. Kirby in pursuit. Franklin found his telescope from behind the Dumpster, where
he'd hidden it earlier.

"I think we made it," Benzer said, wiping his forehead
with a bare arm. A trickle of blood was running down his
forearm from a deep scratch, but he didn't seem to notice.
He kept glancing over his shoulder. "Remind me not to
do that again."

Franklin smiled. "I agree. Too close for comfort."

I gave them my best grin, but still couldn't speak, my
heart was beating so hard.

"Hey!" a voice called from the dark.

The three of us jumped. Patty strode past us, cool as a
cucumber. "Y'all forgot I have to lock the door."

We were staring, openmouthed.

"What?"

"Patty," I said, "you were awesome. How in the world did you know which room I was in?"

"Franklin figured it out. There was only one room upstairs that had the lights on."

"How'd you get out of there? I was scared to death the police were going to show up."

"Nah," Patty said, smiling. "It was nothing. I just took a good look at the sign behind the counter and realized I was at the wrong bed-and-breakfast. He was so relieved to see me go that he didn't ask questions. I walked right out the front door."

Benzer looked me over. "Where's the book?"

I slapped my forehead. "Oh, no! It's still on George Neely's floor."

"You mean we did all that for nothing?" Benzer looked as dejected as I'd ever seen him.

"Well," I said, digging my hand into my shorts pocket, "I did find this."

The three of them gathered around me to read the piece of paper.

"That says *Mayhew* in the margin," Patty said with wonderment. "That's just creepy."

"I told you he was after the gold," I said. "Why else would he have this?"

"Let me see it." Benzer held it up in the glare of the street lamp and began reading. "*Carriage, twenty-one dollars; cookie press, fifteen cents; organ, eleven dollars; slave chest, two dollars. . . .* What is all this?"

I shook my head. "I don't know."

Franklin's watch beeped, signaling it was almost ten o'clock.

"Darn," I said. "We've got to run for it." I folded the paper and put it back into my pocket. We took off like our tails were on fire. Mama and Aunt Sophie were on the porch when we came barreling into the yard.

"You'd better hurry." Mama laughed. "We were just about to call in reinforcements."

"How was the meteor shower?" asked Aunt Sophie.

We all answered enthusiastically and, claiming bathroom emergencies, rushed inside.

"What do we do now?" Patty whispered.

"Yeah," Benzer said, "the list proves George Neely is interested in the house, but we still don't have the book!"

"Shh," I said, and pointed to the hallway. Mama and the rest of the ladies were saying their good-byes. "Maybe there's another way. We'll work it out at church on Sunday."

"Don't forget about the list," Franklin whispered. "George Neely had it for a reason."

I put my hand on my back pocket. I could feel the edges of the paper where it was folded. "I won't," I answered. "He's a part of this. I don't know how, but we're going to find out."

I fell asleep as soon as my head hit the pillow. I'd probably been out for a good two hours when a noise from outside my window woke me. Groggy, I climbed out of bed and peered down through the oak branches. Bertie was standing on the sidewalk, digging into her purse for something. She glanced up as the car that had dropped her off pulled away, and I jerked back, hiding behind the sheer curtain.

I climbed back in bed and lay looking at the cracked ceiling. Our family was so strange. Whose grandmother has two different dates in two days? Both sides of my family tree must be nuts. I wondered if it had always been this way. Maybe Walter Mayhew was just the tip of the iceberg. Maybe if I knew the whole story, I'd find out he was fairly normal for a Mayhew.

I bolted upright in bed. The Mayhew auction list—it had to be from the auction Daddy had told us about—when all of our stuff was sold to the Wilsons. I pulled the paper out from under my pillow.

Carriage, twenty-one dollars; cookie press, fifteen cents; organ, eleven dollars; slave chest, two dollars; iron skillet, one dollar, twenty-five cents; bed, eight dollars. . . . I read the list, twenty-seven items total. I looked closer. The slave chest had a thin, penciled line around it.

Suddenly, it all clicked into place. George Neely had been at the Tate Brothers auction looking for the slave chest that the Wilsons had bought years ago! But he didn't find it because it was just an ugly old painted-over box mildewing in the basement. I sat back against the pillows as the truth hit me. The slave chest that was listed in the auction was sitting downstairs in Daddy's workshop, where I'd been refinishing it for weeks!

For the second time in a matter of minutes, I got out of bed. Standing with my ear against my bedroom door, I heard Bertie's light footsteps go past. I counted the seconds in my head—one Mississippi, two Mississippi—until five whole minutes had passed. Then I started downstairs and made a beeline for the slave chest.

CHAPTER 14

From the diary of Louise Duncan Mayhew
January 1863

As if Mr. Lincoln's war has not taken enough from me, Mother has died. Olivia grieves with me as she knows too well what this pain is like, having lost her own only two years ago. I feel as if I'm trapped in a nightmare with no end.

Daddy's shop was locked, but I found the key easily and pushed open the door. Since my parents' room overlooks the backyard, I couldn't chance turning on a light. Instead, I dragged the table with the chest on it over to the window. The moonlight streamed through the window, and I could see well enough.

I eyed the chest carefully. While I had been working on it, my mind was always somewhere else. So even though I'd spent hours cleaning and staining it, I'd never really examined it.

I opened the lid and looked inside. Everything seemed normal. I grabbed a metal file off of a shelf, and taking a deep breath, I began to poke and prod the wood. Every bird, every piece of fruit was given the once-over, until I reached the portion of the chest with the odd leaf I'd noticed earlier. It was the only flaw in the carving, due to what looked like a wormhole on the edge. I put the tip of the file deep into the space and pushed. A small *click* sounded in the dark room, and I watched, mesmerized, as a panel of the inside wall shifted slightly. Barely daring to look, I tugged at the wood panel. It swung open to reveal a hidden compartment.

I'm not sure what I had expected—maybe gold coins or a treasure map with a red X to mark the spot—but when I put my hand inside, I found a dusty leather-bound book.

"Whoa," I whispered.

I blew the dust off the front cover and found a spot on Daddy's workbench to sit. I leaned against the sill and opened the book.

The diary of Louise Duncan

If you find this, my dear friend
The heartfelt musings I have penned,
Know they belong to me alone,
Until I lie beneath cold stone.
    Louise Duncan

As in Louise Duncan *Mayhew*, my namesake! I felt like jumping up and calling Benzer to come over, but it was three o'clock in the morning, so that was out. I read through the pages, stopping occasionally to figure out the handwriting. I was finding it hard to believe that this was my ancestor. My heart sank as the word *slave* jumped off the page at me.

> *Father does not own many slaves, just Jeremiah, Dode and Singer for the outside work, Molly and Lainey for in the house. Our farm is not large enough to be called a plantation like the Sims' or Johnsons', but still I am proud of its nete appearance. Father had the house painted a month ago and it gleams a beautiful white.*

It took a moment for me to realize she was talking about our house! I wondered if the Sims and Johnsons were related to the ones I knew. From that point on, I read slower, looking carefully for anything that sounded familiar. She mentioned Walter several times—his hope that the conflict could be avoided, then when it wasn't, enlisting to fight. My heart was racing; these people were real!

> *Walter is home! It does not seem possible, yet it is. He rode in with the 8th Calvary yesterday, ate everything Molly and I could put in front of him,*

and locked himself in the library with Silas Whittle who was visiting. I admit I feel a bit confused and shy in his presense. Walter only took a moment to hold my hand, and said nothing of why he was able to come home. I was only able to ascertane his mission by hiding in my usual space behind the bookcase.

I leaned back against the wall. Holy cow! My bookcase! Goose bumps broke out across my arms, and I slowly turned the page.

Oh Diary, he is a hero! A Company traveling nearby have captured a well-known abolitionist. He is wanted in Nashville for helping slaves escape, and while he had none hidden in his carriage, he was carrying a large bag of gold. General Dibrell and his troops are suffering greatly, and need supplies and munitions. Walter has been tasked with guarding the gold until Dibrell arrives and asked Silas to pray for their success in the mission. They are bringing the gold tomorrow and will hide it in the courthouse. I heard him say there is a trapdoor in the judge's chambers, put there in case a judge needed to make a hasty departure. I'm beside myself with excitement. Imagine! I am betrothed to a bonafide hero. I won't sleep a wink!

Some hero! I could hardly wait to see what she thought of her precious Walter once he stole the gold. I stopped and hugged the book to my T-shirt. Closing my eyes, I offered up a quick prayer. "Lord, please let there be some information in here. Please! If this is another dead end, I'll just die!" It was no more dramatic than most of my other prayers, but a strange feeling began to creep up my spine. I found myself feeling almost giddy. I laid the book on my lap and began to read.

Dear Diary,

I can barely write this, as my heart is heavy with sorrow. Indeed, my entire body feels weighted down by grief and I can scarce get my hand to move. But share this I must, or go mad from the deceet. Because of my willfulness, two people are dead and my betrothed is facing imprisonment. I will try to pen this as truthfully as possible, sparing myself no quarter.

The last few weeks had been more bearable than usual. Walter was home, although I understood he could be asked to report to his unit at any minute, and we spent every available moment together. Olivia and I set ourselves to fattening him up, as we were most shocked at his appearance. He had lost a great deal of weight due to a bout of dysentery that I suspect was more horrid than he conveyed. He was very appreciative and a most attentive beau. Still, there was a small part of my heart that I was unwilling to give completely. I told myself it was Walter's serious demeenor that gave me pause, for he had changed much since the last time we spoke. When he and Olivia discussed the deplorable conditions of slaves, they ignored me as if I was a child and if I had had less patience we might have quarreled.

But this was not the entire reason for my reticence. I was reluctant to end my friendship with Brody Kimmel. We'd known each other since childhood, and I was fond of his mischievous antics. I cannot explain why, when engaged to a man of Walter's character, I'd be drawn to a man who's reputation was the subject of much contempt, but I was. I would add that we'd done nothing improper, but that would be a lie and I've promised that I would be truthful. Yes, Brody had kissed me on two occasions, and I had allowed it. I do not deserve Walter for that reason alone, but there is more.

A few days ago, after the floors had been cleaned and the windows (what few still had panes) had been washed, I took a moment to sit on the front porch and rest. Walter had received news that General Dibrell's regiment was approaching and went to greet them. I acted unconcerned, but knew what this news brought. Walter would be surrendering the gold soon and most likely departing thereafter. I was unsure of how that made me feel, and I looked for something else to occupy my thoughts. Perhaps it was fate, or maybe the devil, that caused Olivia to choose that moment to sneak out the backdoor for one of her "errands," but I decided that it was high time I found out what she was up to. I began to follow her at a discreet distance. She walked down the dirt path away from town. It wasn't long before she disappeared into the thick woods of the Stanton property. Had I been walking a bit slower, I would have missed her entirely, but I saw the flash of her bonnet through the trees. The cattle path she followed was familiar; it was the very one I had used many times to meet Brody. That thought had barely passed, when he stepped out into the open. For a moment I thought I had conjured him, and forgetting all about Olivia, was about to shout out a greeting. I was spared that humiliation, when she greeted him instead! They embraced briefly and I felt a pain as deep and as sharp as if they'd taken a knife to my breastbone. I quickly hid among the thick pines.

Oh Diary, why didn't I just confront them? But no, I stayed, listening to them talk quietly to themselves, my heart growing darker and more bitter by the second, even though I could hear nothing of their conversation. Me, with a betrothed, jealous of my cousin and a boy I wasn't even sure that I cared for.

I ran home in tears, thinking the blackest of thoughts regarding Olivia. Not long after, I heard her come upstairs. She paused for a moment at my door, and called my name, but I refused to answer.

Finally, I could stand it no more; I had to see him. I walked (a full hour, Diary, I was insane with jealousy) to where he was building a home. Mr. and Mrs. Kimmel had been so shamed by his refusal to join the war that they had immediately given him a piece of pastureland at the furthest end of their property. His house was almost finished and I found him on the porch, inspecting the handiwork.

"Isn't this a nice surprise?" he said, smiling at me. "In broad daylight, yet? Won't your betrothed be scandalized by your behaviour?"

I gave him my most scornful expression and told him, "My betrothed has nothing to fear from my behaviour ever again."

He smiled and I could see that he was not taking me seriously. "Louise, I swear you've got a real bee in your bonnet. May I ask what's caused your sudden change in demeanor? Has your future husband been upset by the war's turn and made you the recipient of his frustrations?"

I was indignant. "It takes a great deal to upset Walter, and he certainly would not lay his frustrations at my door. He is of a most sturdy character."

Brody laughed. "Sturdy? My, that is high praise indeed."

"You are just jealous that Walter is of such fine reputation, while you are nothing but a flirtatious ne'er do well. Walter has proved himself throughout this horrible conflict."

If I thought I could hurt his feelings, his loud laugh proved otherwise.

"A flirtatious ne'er do well? I suppose that's as good a name as any. But I have to question your portrayal of Walter. If he has proven himself as you claim, why would he be sent home? Perhaps the military is not as taken with Walter as he has led you to believe."

Diary, that was the moment. The moment I would give my life to take back. You see, I stood there, seeing his arrogant face, and was overcome with fury.

"You, sir, have gall talking to me about misleeding someone. If anyone has misled me it was you! I admit that I have been too free with my affection, but do not stand and belittle my betrothed. Walter has been entrusted with a true heroic duty. Under the very noses of the Union, he has been guarding a delivery of gold for General Dibrell."

That gave him pause, but then he shook his head. "I doubt that, Louise. The Union has been over every inch of this County. If Walter had any gold to guard, it would have surely been found by now."

I was so infuriated and told Brody, "You have never given Walter his due, and even now, you refuse to. Walter knows just the place—a trapdoor in the judges' quarters at the courthouse—where they would never think to look. Would you have found such a place? Never!"

Yes, Diary, I betrayed my fiancé and his duty. My temper had gotten the best of me. I did not believe my disclosure would hurt Walter; after all, Brody lived so far from town, and had no interest in the war. Still, a small voice whispered that I should not have done it.

I consoled myself with thoughts that it would all be over soon. Walter soon informed me that his meeting had gone well, and that he would be leaving in a fortnight.

The first sign of trouble came two nights later, when the church bells began to ring. I threw on my robe and went into the hallway. Olivia emerged from her room, a frightened look on her face that I imagined must reflect my own. The thought of Union troops invading our home was never far away, and I could see Father at the door, preparing a weapon. We heard a horse at full gallop enter the yard, and the voice of John Stanton calling out. Olivia and I lit candles and rushed downstairs as Father threw open the door.

"The courthouse is on fire!" Mr. Stanton yelled.

Father hurried to dress, and Olivia, determined to help, followed after him. Coward that I am, I could not go. Muttering that I would stay and watch over the home, I huddled like a scared child in my room. There was no doubt in my mind of what was happening. I had told Brody about the gold, and he was steeling it. That or he had sold the secret to the Union. Either way, it made no difference, I was at fault and Walter would never forgive me. I stayed at my window and stared at the glow coming from town, praying that all would turn out well. At some point I fell asleep for the next thing I knew, the morning sun had made its appearance. Figures slowly appeared in the yard. Father first, then a weary Olivia. I met them at the gate, and they both leened on me, smelling of smoke and sweat.

Olivia clung to me, crying. "Oh, Louise, it's just awful. Brody Kimmel has been killed and Silas Whittle has been shot." She put a hand on my shoulder as if to bring me comfort. "Walter instructed them to take Silas to his house, but they expect the worst." I fainted at that point, my body seeking some relief from the terror I had wrought.

The days that followed flew by as if hidden in a deep fog. I sensed what was happening, yet had no clear vision of the actual events. I had little opportunity to see or speak to Walter as he spent all of his time at Silas's bedside.

General Dibrell sent an officer to assist in whatever way he could, but I soon grew to suspect he was more interested in monitoring Walter than helping the Reverend, and the guilt grew heavier.

It wasn't until the day of Brody's funeral, with Silas fighting for his life, that I confessed my part in the drama to Olivia. I expected her to be shocked, but she just nodded and revealed to me the most amazing news. She already knew! And what's more, she and Brody were not intimate as I had imagined, but rather working together to help some slaves in town.

"Brody was adamant that I tell no one," she

explained to me. "He felt that his reputation would undermine the entire effort."

I lay on the bed and cried. "But I caused his death!"

Olivia lay down on the bed next to me. Her cheeks were wet with her own tears. "Then I share that burden. Brody came to me and told me that he planned to steal the gold back."

"Back?"

"Where do you think the gold came from, Louise? Brody had organized its delivery from our connections in Nashville. I volunteered to smuggle the gold here, relying on the fact that I'm a woman and thus most likely to go unchallenged. It was foolish, since spies were watching, and my companion was searched and arrested. I only managed to avoid detection by sheer luck. When we arrived in town, Mr. Stevenson, the milliner, called me into his shop. By the time I came out, my friend was in leg irons." Olivia wept softly. "I hate this war; we've lost so many good men. I counted the gold as lost, but not Brody." She cried harder. "I should have tried more earnestly to stop him!"

It was too much to grasp. Olivia and Brody helping the abolitionists! "But that's treason!" I said to Olivia.

Olivia placed her hand on my cheek. "Surely, Cousin, you must see the wrongness of this war. Would you condemn Jeremiah, Singer and the others to a life of slavery forever?"

I could feel the weight of it all pressing down on me until I felt that I would go straight through the mattress ticking. Jeremiah, Molly, Singer, Lainey, Dode—I had known them my whole life, a constant reassuring presence. "No," I answered softly. "I don't suppose I would. And the gold was to help them?"

"Yes, and others in the area like them."

I began to cry again. Not only had my indiscretion cost Brody his life, but perhaps others their freedom as well. It was all so confusing. I wanted the best for them, but how would we survive without their help?

We consoled ourselves as best we could, but I knew I would find no rest until I told Walter the truth.

The following day, Father tapped lightly on my door, and with a shaking voice, informed me that Rev. Whittle had died.

I had to stop reading for a few minutes to take it all in. Walter was supposed to have stolen the gold, not Brody

Kimmel. And Louise—how could she have blurted out such a secret? My ancestors were becoming very real to me, and I wasn't sure if I liked any of them.

The sun was just beginning to rise, and a light went on in my parents' room. Daddy gets an early start, even on Saturdays.

"Darn." I shut the lid of the slave chest and carefully closed the diary. If I hurried, I'd be able to sneak back upstairs before Daddy finished dressing.

I'd just gotten back into bed when I heard Daddy go downstairs. I read more by the faint light coming in through the window.

Mr. Stanton gave me the use of his carriage and I made the short drive to the small house that had been Walter's childhood home. A gathering of the church faithful was already there, bringing food and encouraging one another. Silas had lost both of his parents early. Walter, although no blood kin, was as close as a brother.

I found him on the back porch, alone, sitting silent and still as a statue. He shook himself to life, and stood as I approached. We held each other, and despite my earlier determination to give myself no quarter, I must admit, Diary, that I savored it for as long as possible. Tears began to run down my face, but I had no words. I do not know how long I would have stayed in that state, had Walter not placed a loving hand on the cross I wore around my neck. The cross that had belonged to his mother, and which I now knew I was not worthy to wear.

I began to speak, and Diary, I told him everything. From eavesdropping under the stairs, and my fondness for Brody, to my culpability in the burglary of the gold, I spared him none of it. When finished, I sat, waiting for his judgment, not daring to look at his face. A moment passed. Then another. Finally I could stand it no longer, and I placed a hand on the gold chain holding his mother's cross. Lifting it carefully over my head, I held it out to him.

"Dear, dear Louise," Walter said, taking the cross from me. "I am in no place to offer condemnation. If anyone is at fault, it is me."

I was shocked. "Walter, how can you possibly blame yourself? If I hadn't told Brody Kimmel about the gold, he wouldn't have stolen it!"

"Brody didn't steal the gold," Walter replied. "He tried but was too late. The gold was already gone."

Confused, I asked, "But how? Who else would steal it?"

"I was on route to the courthouse when I saw

Brody approach. Something about the way he moved troubled me, and I decided to stay hidden. I watched, amazed as he made his way to the judge's chambers and began to leave with the box containing the gold. I was not quick enough to stop him from setting the courthouse on fire, so I followed, surmising that I would catch him with his conspirators. He walked only a few short yards before ducking into the woods. I was there, watching when he opened the box. I'm not sure who was more surprised, him or me, to find it empty."

"There was no gold?" I whispered.

"Not one coin, only rocks. Someone had beaten Brody to it. I was about to step into the clearing, when a shot rang out, and Brody fell wounded. He managed to get his gun out and shoot once into the woods, before collapsing. The dark prevented me from seeing his assailant. I grabbed Brody and carried him back toward the courthouse. I was hoping to find help, but it was too late. When Brody was found later, everyone assumed he had been shot pursuing the arsonist. The townspeople are calling him a hero."

"But who actually did shoot Brody?"

Walter rubbed his eyes. They were bloodshot and tired, and I was reminded that he had most probably not slept in days. "There are some who believe I did, but I swear to you, Louise, I had nothing to do with his death."

I put a hand on his face. "I know you are incapable of such as this. But who?"

When Walter told me he thought it was Silas, it was too much to believe, Dear Diary.

"But why?" I asked him. "Why would the Reverend do such a thing? Walter, surely you're mistaken."

"I wish I were. As Brody lay there dying, I played it over and over again in my mind. Who knew the whereabouts of the gold? As far as I knew, there was only myself and Silas. As much as I didn't want to believe it, I came to see it as the only logical explanashion. Brody Kimmel had shot into the dark. Silas had been shot. No one else even fired a gun despite the rumors of enemy soldiers in the area. Before he died, Silas came into consciousness enough for me to question him."

I gripped Walter's hand. "What did he say?"

"He confessed. He'd stolen the gold only moments before Brody arrived to do the same. When he saw Brody looking for the gold, he decided to seeze the opportunity. He would kill Brody, and claim he'd seen him with Union soldiers. He knew all about Brody's involvement with the Negroes, *and thought that alone was enough reason to kill him."*

"I don't understand. Then where's the gold?"

"He tried to tell me. I truly believe that, Louise. In the last moments, when he knew the end was near, he tried to tell me. But he was only able to get out one word before dying."

"What was it? What did he say?"

This was it, finally, after everything, the gold! I turned the page, breathless.

"Havilah."

I stared at the page. "You've got to be kidding me." Of all the things he could have said, with his dying breath, it was *Havilah.* Not *in the cellar behind a wall* or even *ten paces past the hitching post*? I'd never heard of a place around here called Havilah. Maybe it was a person. Just my luck. The one time I wanted to hear a preacher ramble on, he couldn't!

From the diary of Louise Duncan Mayhew
July 1863

Molly is needed outside, and it has fallen to me and Olivia to darn our own clothing. My house-dress has been patched so often, it looks like one of Mother's patchwork quilts. With so little food in our larder, our clothes hang on us such that we resemble scarecrows.

***

"Louise, come here and see what I found."

Mama stood in the driveway, straddling a large wooden rocking horse.

"Isn't it amazing? I found it at an estate sale in Cookeville. It's an old German rocking and pull horse. Can you believe it?"

"Uh . . . wow." I yawned as I walked out onto the front porch. I'd stayed up reading the diary until the words had begun to run together. I'd finally given up and hidden the diary under my bed.

"Where's Bertie?" Mama asked, running her hands over the painted saddle. "She'll appreciate this."

"Still sleeping, I guess. I haven't seen her."

Mama placed both hands on her hips, causing her huge belly to poke out even farther.

"C'mon, help me get this inside. It's heavy."

We pushed and pulled the wooden nag onto the porch. As we crossed the threshold, Mama punched the doorbell, setting off "Rocky Top," the UT theme song.

"'Home, sweet home, to me!'" I sang along.

"Mother!" Mama yelled up the stairs. "Are you going to sleep all day?" She smiled at me and winked. "Payback for my adolescence." In a few minutes, Bertie's door opened and she leaned over the railing.

"What is going on down there?" She was wearing a black silk robe with feathers at the neck.

"Come and see for yourself."

Bertie seemed unimpressed. "Lily, what is that pile of firewood doing in the hallway pretending to be a horse?"

Mama frowned. "Very funny, Mother. This is a genuine German rocking horse from the eighteen hundreds. Why are you still in bed?"

"Didn't you hear that wind last night?" Bertie wrapped her robe tightly around her thin body. She started down the stairs and continued, "I couldn't get a wink of sleep for thinking that oak was about to come crashing through the roof."

"I can see what kind of day this is turning out to be," Mama said. "Come on down, and I'll get you some coffee."

We walked into the kitchen, and Mama poured Bertie a large mug.

Bertie took a long sip. "Ahh, just what I needed. So, Lily, is Tucker meeting with the tree fellow today or not?"

"I think he called them yesterday, Mother. He left early this morning so he could get his work done. He's driving Isaac to Knoxville this afternoon. Remember, today's the big tryout for the Volunteers?"

"What?" I asked, turning so fast I bumped the table, spilling coffee on the tablecloth. "I thought that was next week. I promised Benzer that we'd go!"

"I told you the other night it had been changed," Mama said. She picked up a dishrag and began wiping at the cloth.

"No, you didn't!" I was almost in tears. "You think you did, but you didn't. It's another example of your pregnancy brain!"

"Louise, calm down. Your daddy will come home to change—you can still go."

I raced out of the kitchen. "I've got to get dressed," I yelled, "and call Benzer. He'll die if he misses this."

An hour later, Benzer was in my living room, wearing a pair of pressed khakis and an orange UT polo shirt. His dark hair was gelled down flat against his head, and he kept pulling at his bangs as we waited for Daddy to come downstairs.

"Benzini," I said, "if you don't stop pulling at your hair, you're not going to have any left."

"Sorry," he muttered, rubbing his hands down the front of his thighs. "I'm just excited about today." He sat down on the couch. "Okay, tell me again what the diary said."

"I've told you three times."

"I know. I just can't believe there isn't more to it," he said.

"What do you mean? Murder and betrayal aren't enough for you?"

He tugged at his hair again. The ugly scratch he'd gotten last night during the fall was visible every time he stretched out his arm.

"What about Havilah? That's what he said, right, so we just need to find out where it is."

"Yeah, right," I said. "I've never heard of a Havilah around here, have you?"

"No, but we'll figure it out. Maybe he said Pavilah, or Havilou, something like that."

"Maybe," I said, unconvinced.

"Where is it, anyway? Let's finish reading it."

"I left it under my bed. Meet me outside, and I'll run and get it."

Upstairs, I dug my backpack out of my closet and carefully placed the diary inside.

"Lou?" Mom called. "Your dad will be down soon."

"Okay," I yelled. "Benzer and I will be out in the shop."

Benzer was waiting by the side of the house. "C'mon." I motioned him through the gate and closed it behind us. "Sit here. We only have a few minutes." I pulled the diary out of the backpack and opened it on my lap.

"That is so cool."

"I know, right? This is where I stopped. *But he was only able to get out one word before dying. What was it? What did he say? Havilah.*"

Benzer flipped through the pages, scanning them quickly. "Union soldiers, the price of cotton, a funeral. Why isn't she writing about the gold?"

"Wait," I said, stopping him. "Read that one."

Dear Diary,

So much has changed over the past few months. Walter and I are delirious in our joy of one another. We were finally married last month, amid all of the speculation and mystery of Gen. Dibrell's gold. It was a small affair, only Father, Olivia, Audrey and Elizabeth were there. I wore a simple cotton dress, not the wedding dress I'd dreamed of as a young girl, but I missed it not. I do believe I am finally grown!

Soon after our wedding, Walter was cleared of any wrongdoing by his commander. He wanted to tell the truth of what happened, but alas, he couldn't. To do so would implicate me and Olivia. As far as anyone is concerned, Brody and the Reverend were shot trying to stop Union sympathizers from burning the courthouse. Despite the military finding, the townspeople, once our friends, have turned on us. We refuse to care. We have one another, and our family, and our Lord.

Our future is unsure, but still, we find joy in the journey. And many suffer so much worse. Once a month, we take our carriage to Brody's gravestone to aid in the upkeep, and we always find flowers. He is remembered.

As for the gold, we have found no trace. Walter continues to search, but it has eluded us thus far.

Louise Duncan Mayhew

"This is crazy, Lou. The gold was real! I don't know if we're going to find it in time, but I think it's cool you're trying."

"Wow," I said, smiling. "You used your starstruck voice! The one you use when you're talking football with Isaac."

He grinned. "Well, you're not as cool as football, but you're all right."

I was still smiling when we heard Daddy call from the front lawn.

"I'm going to hide this back in the chest so it doesn't get damaged. Stall until I get there."

Mama was standing beside Daddy on the grass. "Tucker, don't drive too fast," she said. "You know how the Cookeville police are."

"I know," he said, leaning down and kissing her on the forehead. "Don't worry."

She drew a sharp breath and put a hand under her belly. "Wow. That was a sharp one."

"Are you okay?" I asked. It would be just like the baby to come early and ruin our day.

"Don't get excited. It was just a kick."

I looked her over. She was wearing a neon yellow T-shirt, and as usual it seemed stretched to its limit. The heat had caused her curly hair to frizz, and the overall effect gave her the appearance of a tennis ball that had been left out in the rain.

I felt so guilty for thinking such a thing that I gave her a big hug.

"Love you."

She hugged me back. "Love you too. Tell Isaac good luck for me."

"Okay."

She stood on the porch, waving, until we were out of sight.

We pulled into Isaac's driveway, and Daddy gave a quick honk on the horn. We were driving Mama's Toyota; Daddy's truck would have been too hot and slow. I would have liked to ride in the back with Benzer so we could talk about last night and the diary, but I knew Isaac and his girlfriend would want to sit together.

Daniella came out of the house looking like an ad in a fashion magazine in a denim skirt and a white tank top. She had an orange scarf tied around her neck.

I looked down at my own jeans and #16 jersey. Maybe I should take Patty up on her offer to go shopping before junior high started.

Isaac and Daniella walked to the car, and Benzer scooted over to make room. I had been so busy looking at what Daniella was wearing that I hadn't noticed Isaac. He was sporting a dark bruise on his cheek.

"Dude! What happened?"

Isaac gave a quick shake of his head and got in the car.

Mrs. Coleman had followed them outside and came to Daddy's window.

"Thank you, Tucker. William and I appreciate you taking Isaac today."

"It's my pleasure."

She held up a hand to wave bye to Isaac. It struck me that mothers sure spend a lot of time saying bye.

The ride was quiet. Daddy can be a man of few words anyway, but when he's driving on the interstate, he gives it full concentration. Isaac stared out the window, headphones on, probably thinking about the tryout. Daniella was asleep on his shoulder. Benzer was quietly reading, and my head was full of all the things I'd learned in the past twenty-four hours.

When we passed a sign proclaiming KNOXVILLE—40 MILES, Daddy pulled off the exit.

"I'm going to fill the tank so we don't have to stop on the way back." He stopped in front of the pump and opened the door. "We'll be back on the road in five."

Tired of thinking about my encounter with George Neely and all the words that rhyme with Havilah (for the record—none), I turned around to talk to Isaac. He caught me eyeing his bruise and took off his headphones. I could hear Metallica coming from the speakers. "It's not a big deal. I'm not hurt."

Benzer looked up from his book. "Was it Drew Canton?"

"No, of course not. It was a couple of guys in my neighborhood. You don't know them."

"In your neighborhood? But why would they hit you?" I asked.

"Because I hit them first?"

"Isaac gets it from everybody." Daniella was leaning her head against his shoulder with her eyes closed. "Either he's in trouble for confronting the coach at the fair, or someone's calling him a chicken for not doing more." She looked like she might cry.

Isaac picked up her hand and held it. "It's okay, baby."

"Tell me who they were. I've got a slingshot at home, and I'm not afraid to use it!" The thought of somebody jumping Isaac made me want to scream.

"I appreciate you having my back, Lou."

"I don't want to make you mad, Isaac," Benzer said, "but I heard Drew Canton is getting a lot of grief too."

"I know. And that makes it worse. I'm not happy; he's not happy. A whole lot of people think it's unfair, and so what? There's nothing that can be done about it."

"Are you nervous about today?" I asked.

He answered in a quiet voice. "A little. I want to do really well. It might be the only time I set foot on the grass at Neyland Stadium."

"You'll do great," Daniella said, grabbing Isaac's hand.

"Yeah, you will," Benzer said. "You're the best player to ever come out of Grey County."

Every time I see the big gold globe, left over from the 1982 World's Fair, that signals our arrival in Knoxville, I get a tingle in my stomach. And nothing compares with going to a UT football game. I've only been a handful of times, but there's nothing I love more than sitting in Neyland Stadium in a sea of orange, screaming alongside 100,000 crazy people.

Since fall classes weren't starting for another month, we had no trouble finding a parking spot in front of the sports center.

"Where do we go first?" Daddy asked.

Daniella pulled a piece of paper from her purse. It looked like it had been folded and refolded so often it was practically see-through. "This says to report to Office 215 to fill out paperwork, and then the tryout will start at one o'clock."

Daddy started up the stairs, followed by Isaac and Daniella.

"Mr. Mayhew?" Benzer said.

"Yes?"

"Since we've got about an hour until it starts, would it be all right if Lou and I walked around campus for a little while?"

I stared at Benzer. I couldn't believe he'd miss a minute of anything that Isaac did.

"I guess so," Daddy said. "Just be sure and be back in time."

"Yes, sir. We'll meet you in the stadium by one o'clock."

Benzer motioned for me to follow him, and we took off at a fast clip toward Volunteer Boulevard.

"What's up?" I asked.

"I can't believe you don't remember," he said, smirking.

"Remember what?"

"That day at the library. The book you wanted to look at, the one that George Neely had in his room."

Benzer was walking so fast, I practically had to run to keep up.

"*History of Grey County in Photographs*," I said. "I remember the book; I was holding it last night when George Neely almost found me. What about it?"

He rounded the corner, still speed-walking. Looking back over his shoulder, he smiled.

"You really should pay more attention to your friendly librarian. Mrs. Hall, remember? She said there was one other copy."

I put both hands on top of my head. "Oh, man! I forgot."

"That's what I've been trying to tell you," he said, pointing to the building looming over us.

"John C. Hodges Library," I read out loud, amazed.

He grabbed my hand. "C'mon!"

Hodges Library looked massive from the outside, and was just as impressive inside.

"We're going to find something," I whispered. "I just know it."

After filling out a registration form at the front desk,

we were pointed to the second floor. It only took a moment to find the book.

We laid the book across a large wooden table, and I checked the index. "No Havilah."

Benzer leaned his elbows on the table. "That'd be too easy."

Side by side, we flipped through the pictures.

"Check out the Square," Benzer said. "It's dirt!"

The caption read, Main Street, Zollicoffer, Grey County, but there wasn't much to it. A sign hung from a weathered-looking wooden building identifying it as a restaurant. Across the dirt street were two structures— a brick building that I thought might possibly be the Five and Dime and a small house surrounded by a picket fence. Standing around in the dirt was a handful of horses.

"This is barely recognizable," I whispered.

"Yeah," Benzer agreed. "There sure wasn't much around back then."

I flipped through the pages. Pictures of cattle, sour-looking men, and the first car to drive through the county were displayed. "No wonder George Neely kept this book. I could look at it all day!"

I turned another page, and my heart skipped a beat. "Benzer! Is that what I think it is?" Staring up at us, looking pristine and white, complete with a young oak sapling in the front yard, was my house.

CHAPTER 16

From the diary of Louise Duncan Mayhew
July 1863

With so many of our able-bodied men gone, the bur-
den of the rebuilding of the courthouse has fallen
to the women. With Walter under suspicion, I am
given many strong looks, I refuse to be cowed, and
do my work along side them. Penance? Perhaps.

"**H**oly cow!" Benzer whispered.

"You got that right," I whispered back.

We were staring at the picture, so close we were practically in the same chair.

"Your house looks really different," Benzer said.

It was true. I'd never seen any photographs of the house
before all of the additions. It looked so much smaller, and
clean. The front porch wasn't sagging, and no paint was
peeling, but there was no mistaking it. There was my bedroom window and the gingerbread woodwork.

"What's it say underneath it?" Benzer asked.

"Just *Flint Street, 1800s.*"

"What are those things in the background, oxen?"

"I guess. Or really big cows. Dad said our property used to be much bigger. It was a farm, remember?"

Benzer turned the page, but there was nothing else. He glanced at his watch. "We've got to hurry." He looked around the library and then picked up the book. "Follow me."

I scooted back my chair, and followed him through the shelves. "Are you thinking about stealing the book?" I whispered. "Don't they put something in them that causes alarm bells to ring when you leave?"

"Shh." Benzer stopped in front of a copier. "Do you have any money?"

I fished out some change from my pocket, but it didn't help. The copy machine didn't take coins.

"Great. Now what?"

Benzer was saved from answering when a boy wearing skinny jeans and sporting a couple of rings in his lip and nose walked up and began making copies.

I nudged Benzer with my elbow. I knew we were gawking, but I couldn't help it. I had barely got permission from my parents to pierce my ears!

Pierced Boy grabbed his copies and was about to leave when I finally had the sense to speak. "Hey," I said. "Where can we get one of those cards?"

"How many copies do you need?"

Benzer held up the book. "Just one."

He motioned for Benzer to put it on the machine, then ran his card and made the copy for us.

We said a quick thanks, and I stuffed the copy in my back pocket. Benzer put the book away, then we ran for the exit.

We made it to the stadium just in time to see Isaac take the field. Daddy and Daniella waved us over to a spot in the bleachers. I tried to pay attention to what was happening below, but too much was happening in my brain. From George Neely, to the diary, Havilah, and now the picture of my house. All the pieces were there; I could feel it. But I couldn't quite figure it out.

We watched for a couple of hours as Isaac lined up against boys that seemed as wide as Dumpsters. But while they were bigger, Isaac was faster on his feet.

Benzer flew to his feet and punched a fist in the air.

"Way to go, Isaac!"

I leaned over to Daniella. "How do you think he's doing?"

She put her sunglasses on top of her head and smiled. "I think it's going really well. He's made three tackles against this guy already."

"So maybe he'll get a scholarship here after all and we can tell Coach Peeler to stuff it!"

Daddy put an arm around me. "Don't get your hopes

up, Lou. Isaac is doing great, but the best kids from all across the country want to play for UT."

"But Isaac needs this! I don't get it. What was the point of coming here if we don't think it will work?"

"It's a chance to be seen, and to find out for himself if he's got what it takes. But Isaac knows getting a scholarship is a long shot. He's got realistic expectations. You should too."

I leaned back against the bleachers. It seemed like every time we took one step forward, we were pushed back three.

A group of cameramen were gathered on the field, filming the action. I could read the letters WBIR-TV2 on the side of a white van parked nearby; a tall antenna extended from the roof.

I looked to where Isaac stood. He had taken off his helmet to get some water, and I could see his bruise clearly. What the heck? I was tired of sitting around and doing nothing. And Pastor Brian had said "faith without action is dead."

"Hey, Daniella, can I have Isaac's stats for a second?" I asked her.

She fished the worn piece of paper out of her purse and passed it to me. "I'm going for a soda," I said, weaving my way past Daddy to the aisle. The three of them were so busy watching Isaac, they barely noticed.

A cameraman with headphones draped over his shoulder was leaning against the stadium wall smoking. He was a faded gray, like the smoke had embedded itself into his skin. A handsome black man with perfect teeth was standing off to the side, arguing with a large woman in a tight red dress. I recognized him as Trevor Bently, the sportscaster on WBIR. I'd never seen the woman before, but she was definitely the one in charge.

"You're getting the same old stuff, Trevor. For God's sake, do something!"

Trevor Bently threw his hands up in the air.

"What can I tell you, Felicia? It's kids playing football. We've seen it!"

The lady glared. "Then do something we haven't seen!"

I was standing, trying to find a way to begin, when Trevor noticed me.

"Hey, kid, you need something?"

"Yeah. Are you interviewing people? You know, human interest stuff?" It was a term I'd heard on television. I wasn't exactly sure what it meant, but every time they showed one, Bertie and Mama cried like babies.

"Sure we are, kid," the lady said. "Whaddya got?"

I pulled the stats from my back pocket. "You see that guy that just blitzed the quarterback? He led the state with tackles. And he was the fastest guy on his team." I glanced down at the sheet of paper. "He was all-state four years in a row."

Trevor Bently rolled his eyes. "Half the kids on UT's team have stats like that. So what?"

A buzzing sound went off inside the lady's red dress, and she pulled out a cell phone. After a brief hello, she moved away and began yelling into the receiver.

I stood closer to Trevor. "Sure, there are boys on the team with stats like that; there oughta be. But it makes you wonder why he's here trying out instead of sitting in the locker room by now."

His eyes narrowed. "What are you getting at?"

I handed him the sheet of Isaac's stats. On one side was a letter from a college requesting information about Isaac J. Coleman; on the other, Isaac had carefully written the year's statistics.

"Isaac found that in Coach Peeler's trash can. We don't know how many other letters Peeler didn't bother to answer or give Isaac. The only reason Isaac has probably gotten any offers is because he and his daddy worked hard sending out tapes."

Trevor read the stats carefully. "This wouldn't be Coach Dan Peeler, by chance? Played for Florida?"

I shrugged. "That sounds right. Isaac said he's always bragging about how he used to play college ball. As if anyone should brag about Florida—ugh."

"That's him. My little brother was on the traveling team with that jerk." He turned around and motioned to the cameraman. "Frank, get over here. I want to interview this little lady for a second."

I smiled. "Is this going to help Isaac?"

Trevor Bently flashed his perfect teeth. "Maybe so. And it'll certainly get Coach Peeler's phone ringing."

We finished the interview just as everyone came walking down from the stands.

"Lou, you missed it!" Benzer said, grinning. "Isaac went through their offensive line like a knife through butter!"

"That quarterback won't forget Isaac anytime soon," Daniella added. She was so happy she was practically glowing.

"That's awesome!" Their excitement was contagious, and we huddled together by the car, waiting for Daddy and Isaac to come out of the coach's office.

Several minutes later, they walked out, clearly disappointed. Daddy had a grim look on his face, and Isaac refused to meet our eyes. Popping open the trunk, he threw his pads inside and slammed the lid.

Daniella was the first to speak. "Oh, baby, you did so well. How could they not want you?"

Isaac rubbed his face as he leaned against the car door. "Oh, they want me. They just don't have a scholarship for me. They said if I could get here, they'd let me walk on, and we'd see about next year."

"But that's good, isn't it?" I asked Daddy.

"It's real good, Lou," he answered, opening the car door, "but tuition, books, and living expenses add up to a small fortune pretty quickly."

"Maybe you could get a student loan, Isaac?" Benzer suggested.

"We make too much for the Pell Grant, and my dad would have a fit if I went into debt. Plus he's not going to let me pay to come here, especially not when other colleges are offering a free ride."

"But you've been accepted *and* you've made the team—at UT!" I said. "There's got to be a way."

Isaac sighed. "To be honest, even if my parents said yes, I wouldn't want to live with that kind of financial strain."

Daddy started the car, and headed toward I-40. I leaned my head against the window and watched the traffic go by in a blur. Pastor Brian said that the love of money is the root of all evil, and that there are more mentions of money than any other topic in the whole Bible, that money doesn't buy happiness. I should tell him that being poor ain't no big whoop, either.

Daddy dropped Isaac and Daniella off first, then Benzer.

"I'll see you at church tomorrow," Benzer said. "Thanks for taking me along, Mr. Mayhew."

"Anytime, Benzini."

As Daddy and I drove home, I noticed how out of place his large hands looked on the steering wheel of Mama's car.

"Dad?"

"Yeah, ace?"

"I thought you wanted to meet with a scrap buyer while we were in Knoxville. Wasn't that why you were heading there?"

"Originally. But I called him, and he wasn't paying enough to make it worth the trip."

"But you took Isaac anyway. That's awesome."

"Isaac is a good kid and a hard worker. I'm just doing what I'd want someone to do for you if circumstances were different."

"Well, I'm glad you and Mama are good too. It feels like everybody's either racist or crooked."

Daddy stopped the car in our driveway. Mama had left the porch light on for us, and I could see a sliver of light coming from upstairs.

"Lou, not everyone in town is like Coach Peeler, or Pete Winningham, for that matter. There are still a lot of people in town who believe in doing what's right."

"If you say so. I'm just glad that you do."

I woke up to the phone ringing off the hook. Mama's voice drifted up the stairs sounding irritated. Turning over, I snuggled further into the sheets. I'd have to get ready for church soon, but for now, I was happy to close my eyes a little longer.

As the phone rang again and again, I opened my eyes,

wondering. A few seconds later, I heard it slammed back into the receiver.

"Louise Elizabeth Mayhew!" Mama yelled.

Springing out of the bed, I raced down the hall to the top of the staircase. Daddy and Bertie had joined Mama and were standing below me next to the phone.

"Yes?" I asked tentatively.

Mama's hands were on her hips, a stance that never bodes well. "Did you give some crazy interview to the Knoxville news last night, calling Coach Peeler a segregationist?"

I pointed at Bertie. "That's what she calls him. I'm not even positive what it means!"

"Then why in the world would you say it? Come down here, please," Mama said. "Looking up is straining my neck."

I trudged downstairs. Bertie put a hand on my shoulder, winking. "Let's build this girl up with some breakfast before you tear her down."

The phone rang, and Daddy took a step toward it.

"Trust me, you don't want to answer it," Mama said.

I sat at the table as Bertie handed me a plate of bacon, scrambled eggs, fried potatoes, and toast.

"What in the Sam Hill were you saying to the television station?" Mama asked.

I chewed my bacon. "They were just there, asking questions." I turned to Daddy. "I showed them Isaac's stats, told them how good he was, how he found his letters in the trash, that sort of 'human interest' stuff."

"Lou, you can't just go on television saying whatever you think!"

Daddy set his cup in the sink. "Honey, what Lou said is true."

Mama stared at him, obviously surprised. "Tucker! There's more to it. She called a man a racist on the local news. Dave Norris, the superintendent, has already called threatening to sue." She poured me a glass of milk and set it on the table, hard enough to cause it to spill over. "We have enough going on without adding a lawsuit to the mix. The whole town is talking about what she did."

"Lily," Daddy said, "Lou's heart is in the right place. What she did is right. Something should have been done about Peeler a long time ago." He picked a UT cap off the chair and pulled it down over his head. "And if Dave Norris calls back, you tell that no-account son of a gun if he ever yells at my wife again, he'll be drinking his dinner through a straw!"

"Here, here!" Bertie cheered.

I put my hand over my mouth to hide my smile.

Daddy kissed the top of Mama's head and left. She sat down in the chair and put her head in her hands. "This family is going to be in the tabloids one of these days, I just know it."

Bertie laughed. "We can only hope!"

The phone continued to ring all morning, until Mama finally unplugged it. I dressed for church in a hurry, and Bertie met me at the door holding her keys. She was dressed to the nines, wearing a bright pink suit, cream blouse, and pink high heels. When she'd suddenly announced she'd be coming, I took it as a sign she must be dying, but Mama said she was just interested in the gossip.

Bertie parked and made a beeline for a group of ladies standing by the entrance. Several people were looking at us and whispering. Obviously they'd seen the news last night.

Benzer, Patty, and Franklin were sitting on our regular pew up front. I sat next to Benzer, and Patty leaned across him to whisper, "I can't believe you were on television last night!"

Holding a hymnal in front of my face, I whispered back, "Forget that. I've got big news."

"Yeah, yeah. Benzer told us about the diary. But you were on TV!" The last was whispered loud enough to cause several people near us to turn and stare.

Benzer pulled a piece of paper out of his pocket and unfolded it. I could see it was the copy we'd made at the library. Patty took it from him and looked it over.

A few minutes later, she handed it to Franklin. No one seemed to know what to make of it.

I listened with half an ear as Pastor Brian started his sermon about some guy named Gideon. "What he wanted," he said, "was a sign from God. He needed proof that what he was doing was what God wanted him to do, so he hung out his fleece."

I peered around the bouffant head of Marie Harbour. A sign? That would be great. I'd missed the part about what a fleece actually was, but maybe God would forget that bit.

The song leader led us in a rousing rendition of "Just as I Am," but I leaned my head on the back of the pew in front of me and prayed.

"So, God, could you give me a sign, something, to let me know whether we should keep looking for the gold, or if we should just give up?" A tear came out of nowhere and threatened to multiply. "I would really hate it, God," I whispered, "but if you want us out of that house, then I'll go. Could you just make that sign obvious?" I opened one eye as everybody began gathering their belongings. "And quick," I added. "Amen."

The gossip about Coach Peeler had put Bertie in such a fine mood that she offered to take us all to the Dairy Barn for ice cream. Franklin, Benzer, and Patty piled into the back of Bertie's Corvair.

Armed with milk shakes, we drove through the town square, all the windows down and the radio blaring.

"I swear, Lou, you really set this town on fire last night. Whoo-whee!" Bertie yelled. "I haven't enjoyed myself this much since Thelma Johnson's dress got stuck in her panty-hose at the class reunion. It's not easy to top a full moon!"

Franklin laughed so hard milk shake came out his nose, which of course made the rest of us laugh hysterically. With my best friends in the car, and a peanut butter milk shake in hand, I was feeling pretty happy.

A big truck was blocking our driveway, so Bertie parked across the street in the library parking lot. The five of us were laughing at something silly Patty had said when a loud whine split the air. Rushing forward, we made our way around the truck. Just in time to see an enormous limb of giant oak, the beautiful oak tree that had been outside my window every day of my life, come crashing to the ground.

CHAPTER 17

From the diary of Louise Duncan Mayhew
August 1863

My days are filled with physical labor I had no idea was possible. Last week, I pulled weeds from the garden till my hands bled. It reminded me of all the times I saw Molly with bandages wrapped around her fingers, and I was ashamed.

I saw it all as if in slow motion: Mr. Rainey at the base of the oak holding a sputtering chain saw, his face red from exertion. His teenage helper stood on a cherry picker, wearing a Rainey Tree Service T-shirt and tying a thick rope around the next limb. I saw Mama leaning on the porch railing and sipping from a tall glass of iced tea. In the middle of it all, my tree was being sawed into pieces.

"Stop it," I yelled, throwing my milk shake on the ground and waving both arms. "What do y'all think you're doing?"

Mr. Rainey turned off the chain saw and smiled at me. He and Daddy have been friends for years. He's a great joke teller, and most times I'm happy to see him. But not today.

"Hey, there, Lou my girl! Look at you, wearing a dress." He put the chain saw on the ground and, pulling a pouch from his front pocket, stuffed a wad of tobacco in his cheek.

"Mr. Rainey," I said, "I hate to tell you this, but you have made a big mistake. You are cutting down the wrong tree!" Mama came and put a hand on my shoulder, but I ignored her. "I don't know who called you, but that tree is perfectly fine."

Mr. Rainey stared at us, a confused look on his face. "That's strange. Your daddy and I worked out a deal. He hauled off some old cars for me, and I was to come over and get rid of this old oak. It is this oak, right?"

Mama nodded. "It's fine, Mr. Rainey. This is just taking Lou by surprise."

"Yeah," I said, my voice dripping with sarcasm, "someone must have forgotten to tell me my favorite tree was about to be murdered!"

"You go ahead with your work," Bertie said, smiling at Mr. Rainey. "It was just a misunderstanding."

I didn't budge. "There was no misunderstanding, Mr. Rainey. That's my tree, and no one is cutting it down."

He turned and motioned for his helper to come down.

"I guess you all need to sort this out. We'll go ahead and take off for our lunch now."

"I'm sorry, Lou," Bertie said, turning to me, "but that tree is dead as disco, and all you are doing is holding up the funeral."

I continued to stand there, getting madder by the second. For weeks I'd been worried about the house, running around like a fool trying to find gold among our mountain of junk, praying for a sign. Well, God had sure enough given me one now—a big, fat "get your behind out of town" sign, and all I could think about was how hateful Bertie was being about my tree.

I reached down and picked up a small branch. "FYI, Bertie, dead trees don't have leaves!" I yelled.

"Lou," Mama said, low and gently, "I know you're upset, but that doesn't give you the right to yell."

"Honey, surely you can see the danger," Bertie said. "That tree, green leaves or not, has been coming down on our heads for months. I can't sleep a wink for thinking it's going to land on my pillow."

"Your daddy grew up with this tree too, Lou," Mama said. "He wouldn't allow this unless it was absolutely necessary."

"Oh, just forget it," I said, tears stinging the back of my eyes. "What does it matter if my tree gets killed? We're going to be out on the street in a few days, anyway."

"What are you talking about?" Mama asked.

"Mama! I'm not stupid."

Bertie tilted her head back, her features immediately softening. "You know about the house, do you?"

"Yes, I do, and no thanks to anyone here. If I didn't eavesdrop, I'd never know anything!"

I flopped down on the grass and squeezed my eyes shut. The thought of moving was so painful, I could hardly breathe.

Mama stood looking down at me. "Patty, will you take Benzer and Franklin in the house for some tea? We'll be in in a minute." She leaned down on one knee and somehow managed to sit on the ground beside me.

Bertie hesitated briefly and then said, "Aw, heck. Why not?" Pink high heels and all, she sat on the grass next to us.

I stretched my dress over my legs and stared up at the tree; only one large branch remained. "I just can't believe it," I said quietly.

Mama rubbed my leg. "Oh, honey, I'm sorry that this is upsetting you. I was sure you were expecting the tree to come down. We've been talking about it for weeks."

"It's not just the tree," I said, my voice quivering. "It's losing the house—it's everything."

"We didn't want to worry you about the house," Mama said, picking up a strand of my hair. "Your daddy has been trying so hard to figure out a way. We felt sure something would come through."

I leaned back on the grass, resting my head on Mama's shoulder. "Isn't there a bank or something that could loan us the money for an attorney?"

Bertie snorted. "Not with that Pete Winningham calling all the shots. He's the major stockholder of the bank. Major Pain in the Butt is more like it."

"It won't happen overnight," Mama said. "We'll make a counteroffer, try to stall. Hopefully we'll get a fair deal out of the house. And it will take a while for all that to work itself out."

"Great," I said, wiping my eyes. "That makes me feel so much better."

I stared up at my house. I tried to see it as just another structure, one with peeling paint on termite-scarred wood, but it was no use. It was my home, and to me, it was beautiful.

Bertie shifted over until I was squeezed tightly between her and Mama. The two of them put their arms around me, and we sat quietly on the front lawn, leaning into each other.

Finally, Bertie broke the silence. "Listen, no matter what happens, we'll be fine, right? You don't lose three husbands without being able to figure out how to land on your feet."

"Mother!"

"Well, it's true," Bertie said with a sniff.

"It may be true," Mama said, "but no one is ever going to embroider it onto a pillow. Couldn't you come up with something a little wiser than that?"

Bertie hugged me harder. "Okay, how about this? Home is where the heart is, and as long as Mrs. Lily Mayhew, Miss Louise Mayhew, and"—she leaned down to talk to Mama's tummy—"Master or Miss Soon-to-be-Named Mayhew are there, then I am home."

"That goes for me too," Mama said.

I hugged them back. "Okay. Me too, I guess."

"Now that that is settled," Bertie said with a grin, "on to more pressing matters."

"Such as?" Mama asked.

"For starters, how do you suppose we're gonna get up?"

"I'll help," I said, standing and holding out a hand to Bertie.

With a quick heave, she was standing next to me, dusting off the back of her pink suit. We each held out a hand to Mama.

She stood, wavered a moment, then immediately bent double.

"Mama, are you okay?" I asked.

She ignored me, still leaning over and rubbing her stomach. Suddenly, a huge gush of water exploded from between her legs, soaking the ground, her pants, and my shoes.

"*Gross!*" I yelled, dancing out of the way.

Mama turned to Bertie. "Mother, you'd better get the car."

"Stop squealing, Lou, and help me," Bertie said, grabbing Mama's arm. "Your mama is about to have this baby on the front lawn!"

CHAPTER 18

From the diary of Louise Duncan Mayhew
September 1863

The men have their schemes, but we are not with-out plans of our own.

I yelled for everybody in the house, and after jumping around like grease in a hot pan, we were able to get Mama changed and seated in the front seat of the car.

Mama leaned out the car window, calm and beautiful in the midst of the excitement. If not for the occasional grimace of pain, you'd have thought she was leaving for a quick drive to the Piggly Wiggly.

She held my hand before taking off. "Get your daddy on the phone. Tell him to meet us at the hospital."

"Can I come, Mama, please?"

She gave my arm a squeeze. "I wish you could, love, but the hospital says you have to be at least eighteen to be in the delivery room."

I frowned. "I miss everything."

Bertie started the car, and Mama let go of my hand.

"Once the baby's here, I'll send somebody to get you. Big sisters can visit till nine."

They started down the driveway, with me, Benzer, Franklin, and Patty waving and following the car all the way down Flint Street.

Benzer and I stared at the stump that used to be my oak tree. I'd changed from my dress to a comfortable pair of jeans. The portable phone was on the porch swing between us, ringing every few minutes with news from the hospital (Mom is fine, still no baby, the doctor says probably later tonight), relatives looking for an update, and more folks asking if that was me on TV last night.

Aunt Sophie was as firmly planted at the hospital as kudzu, so Patty's dad drove over from Sparta to pick Patty up. Franklin had caught a ride home with them, in part I'm sure, to miss seeing Rainey Tree Service, finally and forevermore, kill my tree.

Benzer and I had watched it all, until the branches were sawdust and all that remained was the stump in the middle of the old roots, looking like a prehistoric spider rising from the soil. Now, hours later, the sun sat low in the sky, coating everything with a warm glow.

I looked over at Benzer. "You really don't have to stay."

"So you've said for the hundredth time. I told you, I'm

not leaving." He was still in his best pants, but had taken off his dress shirt and now sat in his tee. His dark hair fell across his eyes, and the sun had turned him a deep bronze.

Benzer flipped through the diary. I'd shown him the chest and its secret compartment. "It's pretty amazing," he said. "I know we didn't find the gold, but it was real."

I nodded. "It's hard to believe."

Benzer nodded. "Are you going to show the diary to your parents?"

"Eventually. I want to keep it to myself for a while."

"Listen to this. *Dear Diary, It's with great joy that I tell you I've received a letter from Walter. It's a testament to his character that amidst this conflict, his chief concern was my welfare.* The date is around the same time as the letter you found."

I moved to sit next to him. "Keep reading."

"*The death of Brody and the subsequent revelations have changed us all in so many ways. My recent endeavors and his support of them are proof enough of that. I will heed his word of caution, for danger is everywhere.*"

"What does that mean?" I asked.

Benzer shook his head. "I don't know. But if it was dangerous, they probably wouldn't want to spell it out for people."

"Just another Mayhew mystery," I said. A butter-fly landed on the tree stump. I tried to look away, but couldn't—it was like the gap in my mouth when I lose a tooth, where my tongue keeps checking to see if it's really gone.

"I'm feeling better," I lied, as if saying it would make it true, "much better already. Moving might be fun."

Benzer raised his eyebrows. "I guess if you're losing the house, there's no need to go to church anymore."

I nodded. "Yeah, but to tell you the truth, I've kinda enjoyed it." I looked over at him.

He shrugged. "I have too. It was nice to fit in for a change."

"What? What do you mean?"

He seemed to struggle for the right word, and I watched, amazed, as his face turned red. "It's hard being different all of the time. I'm already Italian and a Yankee. Do I have to go to a Catholic church sixty miles away too? I just wanted to see how it felt to be part of the town for a while."

I was going to ask him to explain more, but Isaac pulled into the driveway. Benzer and I waved him up onto the porch.

"Why are you so dressed up?" I asked.

"Church. They had a get-together this afternoon to hear about my tryout."

"Were they disappointed that you didn't get offered a scholarship?" Benzer asked.

"Sorta, but mainly everyone was talking about Lou."

"Oh. You mean about the interview?"

"Yes, the interview. What do you think?" Isaac laughed. "I swear, the whole town heard what you said to that reporter last night."

"Man, I can't believe I missed it," Benzer said. "What did she say?"

"A lot of good stuff about me and some really bad stuff about Coach." Isaac gave me a quick high five. "Thanks, Lou. Really. That was cool."

Embarrassed, I played with a stray vine on the railing. "Yeah, well. I have a feeling I'll be flunking PE when I get to high school."

Isaac laughed again. "Probably. But the good news is our phone's been ringing all day with questions about my statistics, and about whether I've decided on a college yet."

Benzer and I both stood straight up.

"That's awesome," Benzer said, a huge grin splitting his face.

Isaac smiled. "It's been a pretty good day."

"So where are you going to go?"

"I don't know. Maybe MTSU or Tennessee Tech."

I slumped.

Isaac looked at me. "Lou, it's not the end of the world— at least that's what I've been told. I guess not every dream comes true." He walked back down the steps to the yard.

We followed him. "Isaac, we want season tickets to wherever you go," Benzer said.

"Sure," Isaac said. "You'll be first on the list." He stopped in the middle of the lawn and ran a hand across the oak stump. "It's a shame about your tree, Lou. I know how much you loved it."

I sighed. "Yeah, thanks."

He bent down; a small twig lay at his feet, its lifeless leaves turned inside out. As he held the twig up to the sky, the leaves took on the orange tone of the sun. Suddenly, in a deep baritone Isaac sang,

> *The oak, he grows in sun and wet,*
> *and mighty branches soon unfold;*
> *When soil and bark and light have met,*
> *to spin their leaves like Havilah's gold.*

The last word hung on the air, floating in the space between the three of us. My skin had turned cold, and I felt the hair on the back of my neck stiffen.

"What did you just say?" I asked in a whisper.

"It's just an old song my great-grandfather used to sing. Probably an old slave tune, passed down."

Benzer and I watched him pull out of the driveway. Finally, I gathered enough sense to speak.

"Benzer," I whispered. I was holding a hand over my heart to keep it from jumping out of my chest and doing a break dance on the sidewalk. "Did you hear what I just heard, or am I dreaming?"

Benzer shot me a puzzled look. "I heard it, but what does it mean?"

I smiled, slowly at first, then big enough to make my cheeks hurt. "It means we just found Havilah! C'mon!" I grabbed his hand and dragged him to the front porch. The diary lay in the swing, and I quickly flipped the pages until I found the entry dated June 1863.

> *Walter will be departing soon, his duties resuming with the completion of this mission. How I dread that day! I believe he senses my distress, for today he brought the most unusual present— an oak sapling. With great ceremony, he gathered my father, and Silas, and with the aid of Jeremiah, planted it in the front yard. He gave an eloquent speech of which I only remember the following: a small thing when nourished and cared for, will take root and grow to great heights. It was rather sweet, and most unlike Walter to be so bold.*

I held the diary out to him. "Check out the date; it's just a few days before the gold was stolen."

Benzer turned the worn pages carefully. "Here's what I don't get. If the reverend buried a big pile of gold somewhere around the tree, wouldn't they have noticed?"

I shrugged. "Maybe they weren't all that smart."

Benzer laughed. "They'd have to be pretty dumb to be

looking for gold and not see a fresh hole had been dug in their front yard."

Laying the diary back down, we went to stand next to the stump. An idea was forming in my brain, and I ran my hand across the wood. "You're right. It'd be hard to miss"—I looked up at Benzer—"unless there was already a hole dug! Where's the copy you made yesterday?"

Benzer pulled the paper from his back pocket again and we held it between us. The photo showed a thin sapling right where the stump now stood. I jabbed it with my finger. "It would be easy to dig the sapling out and replant it. He hid the gold with the tree!"

"That's it!" He circled the stump. "Dang! We'll never be able to dig it out from under this thing."

I crouched down beside what was left of the tree. Deep gouges were cut into the wood every eight inches, all around the base. I'd watched Mr. Rainey use a large drill to make the holes, which Mama said would be filled with fertilizer to speed up decomposition. I put a couple of fingers in the largest one. On one knee, I peered through the hole; Daddy's dump truck was visible on the other side.

"I've got it!" I jumped up and ran behind the house to Daddy's shop. I burst through the door and hurriedly found the keys to the dump truck hanging on the wall.

Benzer stood in the yard watching as I raced back into the yard and climbed on the bed of the truck. "Don't just stand there. Help me with this," I said, pointing to a thick chain coiled like a snake.

"Lou, have you lost your mind?" Benzer asked.

I didn't answer. "Take this end over to the stump. I think it's small enough to go through the largest hole."

"Your daddy is going to kill us. You know that, right?"

I smiled. "No, he won't. Not when we hand him the gold. Now, hurry."

Benzer pulled the chain over to the stump and began threading it through. I picked up my end and attached it to the truck. I'd seen Daddy drag out all kinds of junk clean as a whistle, even though it'd been firmly embedded in years of dirt and briars. It didn't look so hard.

The phone rang from the porch, but we ignored it. The last call had said the baby wouldn't be there for hours.

Once Benzer had the chain completely through the stump, I threw him a metal fastener from the back of the truck. He pinned the chain securely to itself. "Now what?"

I dug the truck's keys out of my pocket. "Do you want the honor, or should I?"

Benzer shook his head. "No way. Your dad yelled at me once for just sitting in the driver's seat."

"Whatever. At least get in here with me."

We climbed into the worn interior. I'd only driven a couple of times in my life, mostly in open fields. But I figured all I had to do was get us into gear and drive forward. Once the stump was out, we'd park the truck back safe and sound. We buckled our seat belts, and I looked at Benzer. "Ready?" He nodded, eyes wide, and I turned the key.

The engine roared to life. I closed my eyes and sent up a small prayer. Grabbing the gearshift like I knew what I was doing, I pulled it toward me. A loud grinding noise shook the cab.

"Push in the clutch!" Benzer yelled.

I glared at him, but didn't say anything. By stretching my left leg as far as it would go, I could reach the pedal. I pushed it to the floor, then moved the gearshift again. This time it slipped perfectly into gear. Tentatively I pressed the gas, causing the truck to lurch forward and immediately die.

"This is going great," Benzer muttered.

"Just shut it, Benzini," I snapped. "If you're not going to help, be quiet."

I started the truck again, and after a few tries, during which Benzer sat perfectly silent, I was able to get the truck going forward. The slack in the chain tightened as I came to the end of the driveway.

I gave the truck a little more gas, but it didn't budge.

"You're going to have to really lay on the gas," Benzer said, looking out his window at the chain stretching behind us. "The roots must be pretty deep by now."

I pushed the gas harder, nervous beads of sweat popping out on my forehead. If this didn't work, or if the gold had been moved, losing the house would be the least of my worries. Losing my behind would be more like it.

The truck strained forward, the chain tight between the bumper and the stump, locked in a tug-of-war.

The engine was whining at a level I'd never heard before.

"C'mon, c'mon, you stupid stump." I pushed the pedal closer to the floor.

The truck rocked backward and forward, pulled in opposite directions.

A very small movement forward caused Benzer to yell, "It's working, it's working!"

I gave it more gas, and the truck moved forward again.

"Almost there," Benzer shouted over the whine of the engine. "Just a little bit more."

I stretched my leg down, pushing the gas to the floor. Suddenly, the stump came flying out of the ground, and freed from its tether, the truck raced forward. I held the wheel, frantically searching with my foot for the brake. We shot across the street, bounced through the ditch on the other side, and flew across the library parking lot, finally coming to rest when we crashed through the brick wall of the adult fiction section. Bricks landed on the windshield, causing what had previously been a small crack to break open and rain glass down into the cab. The engine shuttered and quit.

Benzer grabbed my arm. "Are you okay?"

I nodded. "I think so. Thank goodness for our seat belts!" Opening the door, I slid down to the pavement below.

Benzer's door was under more of the library than mine was, so he scrambled out my side.

"We are goners when they see this," he whispered.

I looked behind us. The oak stump lay on the grass, its roots dangling behind, like a giant octopus caught on a fishing line.

We left the dying truck and ran over to the stump. A gaping hole was now in our yard. Shoulder to shoulder, we peered down into the dark.

"Nothing," I whispered. "Not one thing."

Benzer stared. "I can't believe it. It can't be."

I shook my head, turning to look at the stump. Its gnarled roots were twisted and bent, a massive confusion of wood. Something at the center caught my eye. Barely bothering to breathe, I walked closer. Bending down, I looked at the very underbelly of the oak. The smell of dirt and wood was overpowering. Deep, held in the very heart of the root ball, was what looked like a leather bag. Benzer knelt beside me.

"Is that what I think it is?"

I reached out a hand and touched the material. Old, rotted almost completely through, it gave way under my fingers. Coins fell between the roots, spilling onto the ground in a shiny mound.

I sat, stunned for a moment. My heart was beating so hard I could hardly breathe. I beamed at Benzer and inhaled enough air to finally speak.

"Gold!"

CHAPTER 19

From the diary of Louise Duncan Mayhew
December 1863

*Walter has written that he will be home soon, for
at least two days. I long for more time, as we have
much to discuss. I have changed and there is much
I long to share. Our letters are often stolen by the
enemy, thus true emotions are rarely penned.*

Falling to my knees, I grabbed a handful of coins and
held them up in the evening sunlight. The weight of them
surprised me. They were big too, much bigger than the
silver dollars Bertie gave me every year on my birthday.
A woman's face surrounded by thirteen stars was on one
side, with the date 1853 underneath. I turned one over and
saw an eagle with wings spread over the words *Twenty D.*

"I can't believe it," I whispered. "You're real." Benzer
and I stared at each other, grinning like sharks.

"Let me see one," he said, leaning forward and taking a

coin from the pile. "Wow. They're so shiny. It's like something you'd see in a movie."

"Twenty bucks each isn't bad," I said. "How many do you think there are?"

Benzer crouched beside me, counting. "I've got twenty-two. Ka-ching!"

"There are fifteen in my pile, so thirty-seven total. What's twenty times thirty-seven?"

"Uh, seven hundred and forty, but, Lou, they're probably worth way more than that."

"Really? How much more? Seven hundred and forty is a long way from twenty-five thousand."

"I don't know," Benzer said, "but they're always running commercials on TV about selling your gold jewelry. I think it's based on how much it weighs."

I held out a couple of coins. "These suckers are heavy." The loud whine of an approaching siren cut through the air. "Get the gold," I croaked. My mouth felt like it was full of cotton, and I had to work hard to swallow.

Benzer began scooping large handfuls of coins and putting them in the pockets of his jeans.

"Wait here," I said, racing into the house. In the kitchen, I slammed open the pantry door and grabbed the first thing I could find—a box of Lucky Charms cereal. Ripping open the box, I burst back outside and dumped the contents in Mama's hedges.

"Help," Benzer yelled. He was standing next to the

stump. His pants, bulging with gold coins, hung low around his hips, threatening to drop at any minute. "I can't move!"

The siren rang in my ears, getting closer by the second. Picking up the rotten remains of the leather bag, I grabbed Benzer's arm with my other hand, dragging him to the side of the house. We crouched behind a hydrangea, emptying the contents of his pockets into the cereal box. We had barely finished when a police car skidded to a stop next to Daddy's dump truck.

"Hide this," I said, handing the swollen cereal box to Benzer. He stuck it deep into the hydrangea, where the purple blooms obscured the leprechaun logo. The rotted leather bag joined it.

Peering around the corner, I saw Deputy Lemon from the Zollicoffer Police Department emerge from his patrol car.

"What's the plan?" Benzer whispered.

"I don't know," I answered softly. "Do you have any ideas?"

Benzer shook his head. "Not really. I guess we could hide in the junkyard until he leaves."

Deputy Lemon walked around the front of Daddy's truck, where the engine continued to belch steam. He muttered something into the microphone on his shoulder, but we couldn't hear what he said.

"Do you think he'll take us to jail?" Benzer asked. His eyes were gleaming with what looked like excitement.

"I sure hope not. Daddy is going to kill us as it is." The phone rang from the front porch.

"Should we get that?" Benzer asked.

"And say what? We can't talk right now, the police are here?"

Benzer sighed. "I guess we might as well get this over with. They're going to know it was us anyway."

I held his elbow, panic-stricken. "Wait! What's our story? Why did we pull the stump out of the ground?"

Benzer just shrugged. "We're kids. People expect us to do stupid things."

"Well, don't mention the gold."

"Duh." Benzer rolled his eyes.

We walked around the front of the house and over to the library where Deputy Lemon stood. Bricks littered the pavement at his feet.

"Hey, kids," he said gruffly. "You two see what happened?"

I put both hands in my pockets and stared at the ground. My long shadow lay across the grass, and I saw that it was shaking.

Benzer spoke up first. "Yes, sir. I guess we did."

Deputy Lemon snorted and shot a large wad of spit on the pavement. "Ain't this your daddy's truck?"

I looked up for the first time. A glistening speck of spit was caught on his chin, and I felt a nervous laugh working its way up my throat.

Ohpleasedon'tletmelaughOhpleasedon'tletmelaugh.

"Yes, sir. But he's not home right now."

He tugged at his gun belt, pulling it higher on his hips. "Then who was driving the truck?"

"I was, sir," I said in a quivering voice.

Deputy Lemon gave me a hard stare. "A little thing like you drove this dump truck?" He raised his chin at Benzer. "You wouldn't be trying to take the blame for your boyfriend, now, would you?"

I opened my mouth to speak, but before I could get out the words, he snorted again. I watched him work his mouth round and round, finally pursing his lips and sending a huge loogie sailing through the air. It landed right on the head of the William Shakespeare statue the library had installed last year.

I clamped both hands over my mouth, but it was no use. I started laughing—tears-down-my-face, shoulder-shaking, doubled-over laughing. Benzer held it for a moment, then he burst into huge guffaws.

"You two think this is funny?" Deputy Lemon asked.

I laughed harder. "No, sir. We're sorry."

"Well, if you're not now, you're going to be. Destruction of city property is no laughing matter. Is your mama home?"

I shook my head no, too afraid to speak. Tears were still streaming down my face from laughing so hard.

Deputy Lemon spit again. "Is there anybody with any sense over at the Mayhew house?"

"No, sir, not for years now," Benzer said, continuing to laugh.

We couldn't control ourselves. It was as if all of the emotions from the day—Isaac, the tree being cut, Mama going into labor, us wrecking the truck and finding the gold—had melded together into a giant ball of craziness that had to get out.

"I bet you won't be laughing when your parents get ahold of you!" Deputy Lemon said. His face was as red as Bertie's pants, and stretched just as tight. He pushed the Transmit button on his radio. "Dispatch, this is Deputy Lemon, come in, please."

Even standing under his angry stare, we still couldn't stop giggling.

"Lou, stop it!" Benzer whispered, his throat catching.

"I'm trying."

The radio squelched back. "Yeah, Warren, go ahead."

"I've got an 11-82 at 81 Flint Street."

"Can't you just say it was a traffic accident? Honestly, Warren, I don't have time to look up all of these codes."

"You need to send a crew over to mark off the street. And you better have someone inform Mrs. Hall she's got a dump truck in her library. Over."

The radio squelched again. "Are your legs broken? Where am I going to get a city crew on Sunday afternoon? Use the cones I know you have, out of your trunk." The radio fell silent. We were waiting for Deputy Lemon to respond, when the radio squawked back to life. "Did you say 81 Flint Street? I just got a call from Tucker Mayhew, asking me to send somebody to check on his daughter. They're in the middle of a delivery, and she's not answering the phone."

Deputy Lemon cleared his throat. "Uh . . . 10-4 on that; I've got her and her accomplice standing right in front of me."

"Accomplice! Warren, isn't she about twelve? Her and Macy Elizabeth were in Brownies together. Get those kids over to the hospital so her parents can stop worrying."

Deputy Lemon grumbled into the microphone, but motioned us into the backseat. I was starting to feel sick from the stress of what we'd done. I put a hand out to roll down the window, but the handle had been removed.

The deputy slammed his door, and we were off, siren still blazing.

Deputy Lemon escorted us into the glaring light of the hospital entrance. Aunt Sophie, Bertie, and various relatives met us in the lobby.

"Well, look what the cat drug in. Where in the world

have you two been?" Bertie asked. She looked perfectly at home in the center of all the excitement.

"Where's Daddy?" I asked, dodging the question.

"He's with your mama," Aunt Sophie answered. "The baby's coming right now." She was trembling with excitement.

"Thank you, Deputy," Bertie said, putting an arm around my shoulders. "I hope these two were behaving themselves." She winked at Benzer.

"Bertie, please," I groaned.

"As a matter of fact, ma'am, I do need to talk to their parents. Is Mr. Mayhew available?"

Bertie smiled. "Talk to them about what?"

"Well," Deputy Lemon said, appearing to wait for a pause in the noise, "seems the little one was driving Mr. Mayhew's dump truck, and it ended up crashing into the library."

The room was suddenly quiet. Bertie tightened her grip on my shoulder. "And by 'little one' you mean my granddaughter?"

"If that's who you're holding. She confessed."

Bertie turned me around to face her. "Is that true?"

"Yes," I said, "but we have a really good reason."

"We?" She turned to Benzer. "I guess you were in on this too."

"Yes, ma'am."

"Louise Mayhew! Have you lost your ever-loving mind?" Aunt Sophie wailed. "And with your poor mama in labor."

"Can it, Sophie," Bertie said. "Accidents happen. Or do I need to remind you of your marriage to Henry Porter?"

"Mother!"

"Deputy," Bertie said calmly, "I'm sure Tucker will rectify the situation with the library at the first opportunity. But as you can see, we're in the middle of an important family event."

As if on cue, Daddy staggered through the swinging doors. His hair was going in all directions, and his face was the shade of biscuit dough.

"It's a boy!" he announced. "Eight pounds, five ounces. Mother and baby are just fine."

The room broke into applause and he smiled, giving us the thumbs-up for a moment, then disappeared back into the depths of the hospital.

Deputy Lemon handed a ticket to Bertie. "I'll call on Mr. Mayhew on Monday."

That was all I needed to hear. This time Monday, Daddy would be so happy about the gold, he'd probably forget all about the truck.

Everyone started to leave after hearing the good news, but Benzer wanted to stay, mainly to delay the conversation between his parents and Deputy Lemon. Bertie was able to convince him to get it over with.

Then it was finally my turn to go in and see Mama. She lay in the bed, looking tired and pale, but happy. "Lou, come and look. Isn't he darling?" She held out a hand motioning me to the bed.

I peered over the covers. She was holding a small bundle, wrapped up like a mummy, against her chest. I wondered how he could breathe.

Mama pulled the thin blanket away from his face. "Hey, little guy. Meet your big sister, Lou."

I stepped closer, and a tiny little face peered back. He had goop on his eyes, and his skin was blotchy; his dark hair was matted against his head, and for some reason, I wanted to burst into tears.

"Hi," I whispered, my voice shaking, "I'm Lou. What's your name?"

"We haven't decided on that just yet." Daddy's tired voice answered from the corner. I'd been so intent on Mama and the baby I hadn't even noticed him sitting there.

Bertie leaned over my shoulder. "Let me have that child for a second." She gently took him from Mama, rocking him back and forth.

Daddy stood and came to watch them for a moment, then put a hand on my shoulder. "Lou, I hear you and Benzer had an accident today." His voice was gentle, but firm.

"Oh, yes, we did," I said, getting excited. "But wait till I tell you why. You're never going to believe it."

"Yeah, I'd like to hear how my truck ended up knocking down the library wall with a stump tied to the bumper."

"Lou, Tucker? Can we save all this for tomorrow?" Mama leaned back against the pillows, wincing.

"Sorry, Lily," Daddy whispered, going to hold her hand. "You just get your rest, now."

"Okay," I said, disappointed. "I guess tomorrow would be better."

Bertie handed the baby back to Mama. "You sure you don't want me to spend the night, Tucker? You're awfully tired to be helping feed a baby at two A.M."

Daddy smiled. "We'll be fine."

I picked up Mama's hand from the bed and kissed it. "I love you, Mama."

She put her hand on the side of my face, cupping my jaw. "I love you too. We'll see you tomorrow."

It was dark outside by the time we left. I practically skipped out to the parking lot with Bertie. Having a brother was already better than I'd imagined. I couldn't wait to tell him the story about the time his awesome big sister found some gold and totally saved his house!

CHAPTER 20

From the diary of Louise Duncan Mayhew
January 1864

Walter's visit accomplished much. While Father would not hear Olivia and I speak of manumission, he did Walter the courtesy of listening. Father finally agreed to put the slaves' freedom in his will, but it was not until Jeremiah and Dode promised to stay on, and swore not to join the Union. Olivia complaned bitterly that such an agreement undermined the issue, but that didn't stop Jeremiah from his happiness. As for our other endeavors, Walter was not as supportive as I had hoped. Being away, he was reluctant that we endanger ourselves, and the fact that my father remaned unaware also chafed. Still, he did not forbid it.

I tossed and turned in bed, finally getting up at the first signs of daylight. I padded down the hallway to Bertie's room and eased into bed beside her.

"Hey, Lou," she murmured, "what are you doing up so early?" She had a scarf tied around her hair and smelled vaguely of Mary Kay moisturizer.

"I can't sleep," I answered. "When will Mama be home?"

Bertie yawned. "I believe they have to keep the baby at least twenty-four hours, so it'll probably be this evening."

"That late?" I sat up in the bed. "Bertie, I really need to talk to everybody."

"What's so all-fired important? Besides, if I'd stolen my daddy's truck and destroyed the library, I'd be a little less excited to see my parents." Bertie stretched her arms over her head. "Do you have a reasonable explanation, or should I just say my granddaughter's touched?"

I threw myself back onto the pillows. "I have a great explanation. That's why I need to talk to Mama and Daddy. Ooooh," I squealed, "a family meeting. I'm going to call a family meeting."

"Oh, Lord. You think that'll help when your Daddy sees what you did to his truck?"

"Just wait," I said, getting excited about the idea. "You'll see. I'm going to call Benzer and Franklin and Patty, and get them to come too."

Bertie yawned again. "Wonderful, that's what we need. More people in the house." She climbed out of bed and came around to my side. Grabbing my hand, she pulled me off the side of the bed. "You start the coffee while I find the phone. After breakfast we're going to clean this house from one end to the other. People will be all over us like ants on a gumdrop."

"Fine," I grumbled. "But this time tomorrow, things will be very different. And I want first dibs on a maid."

Bertie laughed. "Child, if you think you're getting a maid, you are touched. Now let's get ready for your brother's homecoming."

I moved the broom back and forth. I could see the hydrangea bush that was hiding our loot, and I had to make myself stay on the porch. I'd managed to get the diary and hide it back in my room last night, but I hadn't had time to bring in the gold before Bertie made me go to bed. I'd already checked three times to make sure it was still there.

The city had sent out a group of workers to begin putting the library back together. They picked up bricks and hung a blue tarp over the hole where the wall had been, while Mrs. Hall flitted around like a bee having pollen withdrawals. I'd watched from behind the parlor curtains as she'd carried on with the mayor, pointing and waving toward our house. Luckily, they hadn't come over to demand an explanation.

I stared at the hole in the yard. Even though it had given us the gold, I still hated that the tree was gone. My house seemed naked without it. Isaac had come by and managed to get the dump truck over into our driveway, so I was hoping it was still drivable. I didn't know how much the gold was worth, but paying lawyers, rebuilding the library, and buying a new dump truck seemed like a lot.

"Lou, quit lollygagging and get the front porch swept. People will be here any minute," Bertie barked from the house.

"Good," I yelled back. "Maybe they'll bring lunch!"

Bertie walked out the side door. She had on her cleaning outfit—a pair of blue jeans, a crisp white shirt rolled up to the elbows, and a necklace made of large red beads.

"There's some leftover pot roast in the fridge, Miss Martyr. Just don't make a mess in the kitchen. I spent all morning scrubbing out the sink."

I warmed up a plate in the microwave, then snuck it upstairs to eat in my room. Bertie had kept me so busy I hadn't had time to call Benzer. I wolfed down the food, then climbed into my closet with the portable phone.

"Jailhouse," he answered.

"Very funny. Why haven't you called? Did your parents freak out?"

Benzer ate something crunchy into the receiver. "Sort of. Mama cried. She said I was going to end up a juvenile delinquent."

"Oh," I said, leaning against the closet wall. "What are you eating?"

"My own concoction, jalapeño and vinegar potato chips. They're awesome."

"They sound disgusting. Did they ground you?"

"Not yet. Dad said he would wait until he could talk to your dad. I told him that he'd know soon enough why we did it."

"Lou, where have you gotten to? We've got to put the sheets on the crib!" Bertie yelled up the stairs.

"Coming!" I lowered my voice to a whisper. "Listen, I've called a family meeting. I want to tell everybody tonight. Can you and Franklin find a way to get here? Bertie says Aunt Sophie and Patty are bringing Mama and Daddy home from the hospital. We can show them the gold and everything."

Benzer ate another chip. "Yeah, I can be there. My parents said I have to apologize to your dad anyway. By the way, I checked out the gold online. You're not going to believe what it's worth."

"What do you mean, you 'checked'? If you told anyone, I'll—"

"Relax." Benzer crunched. "I did a search on Civil War gold. A site came up with gold pieces just like the ones we found."

"No way!"

"Seriously. Guess what they get for one piece?"

"Louise!" Bertie yelled again.

"I swear, she's going to dust and vacuum me to death. How much?"

"Eleven hundred and seventy-five dollars!"

"A piece?" I choked. "You have got to be kidding me. There's thirty-seven pieces of gold in that box."

"The way I figure it, it's way over what you need."

"*Wow!* Come early and help me figure out how to move the gold. It looks like it might rain, and I don't want the box to disintegrate."

"LOUISE ELIZABETH MAYHEW!"

"I've got to go," I whispered. "Don't be late. And bring the information about the gold."

"Don't worry. I wouldn't miss this for anything."

The rest of the afternoon crawled by. The doorbell rang every half hour, announcing someone holding a casserole at the front door. If they weren't plying us with food, they were staring over their shoulders at the library construction.

"You sure know how to make news," Bertie said, putting the third casserole in the fridge. "They still haven't gotten over your impromptu news conference with the Knoxville television station and then you go and destroy the library. What are you going to do next week, toilet paper Pete Winningham's office?"

I winked. "You never know. I just might."

Bertie placed a hand on her hip and laughed. "Bless my heart! I think you're getting to be right sassy."

I put a hand on my hip, imitating her. "With you as a grandmother, could I be anything else?"

"They're here!" Aunt Sophie's voice blasted from the porch. "Come and welcome the newest member of the family!"

Franklin and Benzer jumped up from the dinner table. They'd been gorging on casseroles for the last two hours. Bertie and I moved quickly, beating them to the foyer.

Mama held the baby, while Aunt Sophie carried in a box of diapers. Daddy had one arm under Mama's elbow, guiding her gently into the hallway. Patty followed them in, struggling under a huge flower arrangement.

"Mama, Mama!" I said, squeezing her around the middle.

"Don't hug too tight, Lou," Daddy said. "Your mama is still sore."

"I'm okay, Tucker," she said. "Let me hold my two children for a second."

"I am so glad you're home," I whispered.

Mama stood hugging me with one arm and holding the baby with the other.

"Guess what?" I said. "I've called a family meeting."

"So I heard. I can't wait to hear your news."

Aunt Sophie put the suitcase down on the steps. "Whew. I am worn plumb out."

"Yes," Bertie said, "just imagine how you'd feel if you'd actually given birth. Here, let me see him, Lily," she said, moving to get the baby. "You and Tucker have been hogging my grandson all day."

The group buzzed around, everybody taking turns holding the baby. I hopped from one foot to the other, anxious to tell everyone the news. Benzer and I had kept finding the gold a secret from everyone, even Patty and Franklin. We'd traded the Lucky Charms box for the slave chest and had brought it inside earlier. It was hiding in the parlor behind a wingback chair.

Mama managed to notice my distress. "Okay, everybody, let's sit down in the den. Lou's been waiting all day to tell us something, so let's give her the floor."

"No, no, not the den. Let's go into the parlor—it's for special occasions."

"Oh, my." Aunt Sophie laughed. "This is going to be good."

Everyone settled in while Benzer and I went to stand in the front of the room.

"Goodness," Bertie said, "I hope you're not announcing your wedding plans. Even I think you're a little too young."

"Bertie, please!" Mama said.

I cleared my throat to speak. "Umm. Okay, here goes."

Benzer and I walked over to the chair and, working together, lifted the slave chest onto the coffee table.

"Lou, honey, is that the box you've been working on?" Mama asked, taking the baby from Bertie. "It's beautiful."

I stood quietly, trying to catch my breath. Now that the moment was here, I didn't know what to say.

"Go ahead," Benzer whispered.

"What is it, Lou?" Bertie asked. "Is something wrong?"

"Nothing is wrong," I said to the room. "Everything is great." With that, we opened the chest and sent thirty-seven shiny Liberty Head gold pieces spilling across the table.

Benzer threw both hands in the air like he was calling a touchdown and cast a huge smile at the room. "Ka-CHING!"

CHAPTER 21

From the diary of Louise Duncan Mayhew
March 1864

A notice has been circulated in the area: "Any person who shall harbor or conceal any fugitive from service or labor, escaping from one state into another, so as to prevent his discovery and arrest, after notice or knowledge that he was such a fugitive, shall be subject to a fine not exceeding $1,000, and, on indictment and conviction, to imprisonment not exceeding six months, and shall forfeit and pay, by way of civil damages, to the party injured, the sum of $1,000 for each fugitive so lost, to be recovered by action of debt.—Fugitive Slave Act, September 18, 1850, 9 Stat. 462."

I can hardly walk through town for my legs tremble so.

A stunned silence filled the room, then Franklin and Patty jumped to their feet shouting, "You found it!" We hugged and laughed, and I handed them pieces of gold. Franklin shook his head back and forth, saying, "Extraordinary, extraordinary."

It took a few seconds for us to realize that none of the adults were speaking.

Mama and Daddy were looking at each other, puzzled expressions on their faces.

Aunt Sophie's mouth hung open. Even Bertie seemed to be at a loss for words for once.

Daddy finally broke the silence. "Lou, what is this about? Where did you get that money?"

The story came tumbling out, from the prayer for something exciting to happen to the Tate Brothers auction where we'd found the chest, and how I'd found the diary. Benzer and I explained why we'd used Daddy's truck to pull up the stump and how we'd had to hide the loot again before Deputy Lemon saw it. Everybody got in on the story. Patty kept saying she'd helped dig in the yard, and Franklin nodded and smiled and generally acted like he'd known we'd find the gold all along. Thankfully, no one got carried away enough to tell about breaking into George Neely's room.

Daddy pinched the spot at the top of his nose between his eyes. "Now, tell me again how you knew the gold was under the stump?"

I sat down on the edge of the coffee table. "The reverend's last word was 'Havilah,' which Franklin found means 'land where there's gold.'"

Franklin beamed. "I just searched for it on the computer; it was really no big deal."

"Anyway," I continued, "that really didn't tell us much. But while y'all were at the hospital, Isaac came over. As he was leaving, he sang an old song about an oak tree and its leaves being like Havilah's gold."

"So you decided to pull up the stump," Daddy said. He was not looking as friendly as a person might, considering his house had just been saved.

"Well, yeah," I answered. "We have to pay the lawyers, right?"

Bertie leaned forward and picked up a piece of the gold. She held it up to the light. "This says twenty dollars," she said. "What do you suppose it's really worth?"

Benzer grinned, pulling a sheet of paper from his front pocket. "I found a coin dealer online selling a piece just like this," he said. "He was asking eleven hundred and seventy-five dollars. For one piece."

Everyone sat still, digesting the information.

"Umm." Aunt Sophie cleared her throat. "And how many pieces did you say are in that pile?"

Benzer and I had already done the math. "Thirty-seven. Worth over forty-three thousand dollars," I told them.

Bertie gasped. "Good Lord, we're rich."

Everyone laughed—well, everyone except Daddy. He sat next to Mama on the couch, staring at the gold coins. I started to get an uneasy feeling in my stomach.

"What is it, Daddy?" I asked.

He looked around at us all. "I was just wondering who the gold actually belongs to."

"What do you mean, Tucker?" Bertie asked. "I've heard the story about the gold a hundred times. Walter Mayhew was guarding a shipment, and it was stolen."

Daddy stood and walked around the room. "If the government was sending down a shipment of gold, surely there would be more than thirty-seven pieces." He turned to look at me. "What's the story, Lou?"

"It wasn't actually a government shipment," I said. "Louise's diary said the gold was sent to a couple of people helping slaves escape, but some soldiers confiscated it."

"What happened to the sympathizers?" Bertie asked. "Terrible things happened to people who helped the slaves back then."

"One of them was arrested. The other one was Louise Mayhew's cousin Olivia."

Daddy looked at me, his eyes wide with surprise.

"That's why Brody Kimmel got shot. He was working with Olivia and tried to get it back." I looked around the room. "Walter didn't kill him, the Reverend—Silas Whittle—did."

Franklin beamed. "Imagine! My ancestor, killed in his effort to be an abolitionist. That's really something!"

"Wow," Bertie said. "This is all very interesting. But

I want to know how much is going to be left over after taxes."

Daddy sighed. "Don't start spending it yet, Bertie. I'm not sure we're going to be able to keep the gold."

"*What?*" five voices yelled at once. Me, Benzer, Franklin, Patty, and Bertie.

"Daddy," I said, "what are you talking about? We have to keep the gold. It's how we're going to save the house."

"I don't think it's that simple, Lou. It's not our money."

I stared up at the ceiling. "God, you have got to be kidding me! I prayed to you, I listened to you—are you just going to sit up there and let him do this?"

"Lou, stop being such a drama queen." This from Aunt Sophie, the woman who called 911 over carpal tunnel in her wrist.

"Why?" I asked. "Why can't we keep it?"

"It's not ours," Daddy said slowly, like he was talking to the baby instead of me. "And that gold was the ruin of Walter and Louise Mayhew."

"But the money was stolen from Aunt Olivia and her companion. So as her kin, why couldn't we keep it?"

Mama leaned forward and touched the diary's leather binding. "I can't believe you found this diary. That in itself is amazing, Lou."

"It is pretty cool," I said.

Patty sprawled on the floor next to me. "If we don't know who it belonged to, what are we supposed to do? Give it back to the Union army? Are they even still around?"

"Over my dead body," Bertie said. "And you're signing up to volunteer at the museum, Patty. You've got some history to learn."

Daddy crossed his arms and leaned against the wall. "Louise, do you understand what the gold was for?"

The rain that had been threatening all day let loose and pounded on the roof.

I hadn't realized I'd been holding my breath until I exhaled. I picked up the diary and started flipping through the pages. "It says that until the soldiers found it, Olivia and her friend were going to use it to help slaves escape. That's why Brody Kimmel was trying to get it back. Olivia was pretty torn up about it when she told Louise."

Daddy sat down on the arm of the couch and put his hand on Mama's shoulder. "Your whole story is pretty remarkable about finding all this. And if you say that a higher being brought it all about, well, I guess I'm inclined to believe it. Have you given any thought as to why you might have found the gold now?"

"It's what I've been saying—it's to save the house."

"Well, what if it wasn't to save the house? What if there was some other reason?" Daddy asked.

"Yeah," Bertie said. "Maybe God thought it was time the library got a new wall."

"Mother, be serious," Mama said.

Bertie snorted. "Surely y'all aren't planning on giving the gold away because of something that happened that long ago. As terrible as it all was, ain't a bit of it our fault. None of us was even living! Besides, there's not a soul that cares about that stuff anymore. People got more on their minds than some old tale about this family. Heck, we've got enough recent stuff to keep them talking for another hundred fifty years. What's one more thing?"

"Daddy, the gold solves all our problems. There is no other reason." I stared at him, begging. "You promised, remember? You said that you'd do everything in your power to help us keep the house!"

He shook his head. "Lou, I don't want to lose the house either. But something just doesn't feel right to me."

I looked over at Benzer, who just shrugged as if to say, "Parents. What can you do?"

"This can't be happening," I said. All of this for nothing? No way. I dropped my head in my hands. If I started crying now I'd die of embarrassment.

Daddy leaned down and picked up my hand. "Maybe Louise and Walter never even looked for it." He smiled gently. "It's way too much trouble figuring out what to do with it."

I picked up the diary from my lap and turned to a page in the back. "*Despite Walter being cleared of any wrong doing, there are those in town who still look upon us with suspicion. We carry on despite the stares. There was a time Walter would have given the gold to his regiment out of duty, but no longer. Duty to the Confederacy comes second to one's duty to God. William Wilberforce said, 'You may choose to look the other way but you can never say again that you did not know.' We do know now, this war has taught us much, and were we to find the gold, I need look no further than the impoverished negro settlement to know how we would use it."*

"They were going to give it away too?" Bertie asked. "This family has always been crazy."

"They weren't crazy—they were doing the right thing. Lou," Daddy said, "no matter what we decide, you found the gold and cleared Walter's name. That should make you feel better."

I frowned, not sure who I was madder at, Daddy or God. "Not as much as you might think," I muttered.

"It is rather remarkable," Franklin said. "Wasn't Walter a captain? I'd love to read that diary, Lou. I'd be interested to see how he could change so much."

"People got their fill of war pretty fast, Franklin," Bertie said. "One out of every three Confederate soldiers said to heck with it and deserted. Glad I missed it. I don't want any part of anything that makes you crazy enough to part with gold!"

Thunder crashed outside as the rain became a full-force

storm. "Maybe we'll get a tornado," Patty said worriedly. "Nothing would surprise me about this day."

We didn't get a tornado, but the weather was rotten enough for Daddy to suggest everyone spend the night. I wasn't sure if it was the weather, or he was just too tired to deal with taking everyone home. Aunt Sophie had left her car at the hospital, and all it took was a promise from her to help with the midnight feedings, and Daddy was making Benzer and Franklin a pallet on the living room floor.

"If I hear one creak on those stairs, you two boys will be wishing for a tornado."

"Yes, sir."

Patty and I snuggled together in my bed. I was glad her tanner had faded to the point she no longer smelled funny.

"Feeling better?"

"Not really."

"You sure pitched a fit earlier," she whispered. "Mama said if you get violent to come and get in bed with her. Are you going to yell at God some more?"

I pulled the covers under my chin. "I would if I thought it would help." I stared at the ceiling. "But Daddy's got me thinking," I said. "He's right. It wasn't Walter and Louise's gold. I hate to say it, but maybe we shouldn't keep it."

"Wow," Patty said. "I can't believe you're saying that."

"Me either, but remember what Pastor Brian said my

first day at church? He said we all have a purpose, even kids, and we don't have to wait to grow up to be used. Maybe I found the gold so that I can do something that Louise and Walter couldn't."

Patty blew a curl off her forehead. "I still think it's stupid. They were going to give it to the freed slaves. What are you supposed to do, look for their great-grandchildren?"

I sat up and stared at Patty. "Oh my gosh!"

"What?"

"Wait here." I threw the covers off and jumped out of bed. My parents' light was still on, and I burst into their room.

"Lou!" Daddy said. "What in the world?"

"I know what we can do with the gold," I said. "I know the plan!"

"I'm sure it can wait until the morning. Your mama just got the baby down."

"It's okay, Tucker," Mama said. "Go ahead, Lou. What do you want to do?"

I sat on the edge of the bed. "Can we give it to Isaac? So he can go to UT?

Daddy looked thoughtful, then grinned. "Sure. I couldn't think of a better use, myself. I'll call him first thing tomorrow. Now, get back to bed, it's late."

"Okay." I headed toward the door.

"Lou," Daddy said.

"Yeah?"

"I know we say this a lot, but we are proud of you. That was a tough decision."

"You know Mayhews," I said softly. "We're made of steel."

Patty and I lay still, listening to the sounds of the house settling. I'd filled her in on my idea for the gold, and now I could tell she was drifting off to sleep.

"Patty?" I whispered.

"Yeah?"

"If I tell you something, do you swear you won't tell?"

Patty rolled onto one pointy elbow and yawned. "Sure."

"Okay," I said, whispering. "I think Benzer is kinda cute—arggh," I screamed into my palm.

"Uh, duh. You've been totally crushing on him for the last year."

"I have not!"

She lay back down. "Of course you have. And he follows you around like a love-struck puppy. Geez. How can you not know this?"

I could feel my face turning red in the dark. "Really?"

"Yes, really. Now, can we go to sleep? I need my beauty rest. Some of us don't have boyfriends yet."

I rolled over and closed my eyes. The thought of leaving the house and going to a new school still felt like a giant weight pressing on my chest. So why did I have a huge grin on my face?

Bertie made a big deal about breakfast, even going as far as to drive to the Grey Motel to bring back a platter of their biscuits and chocolate gravy. Patty and I came downstairs in our robes. Technically they were both mine, but she wore the same one every time she spent the night, so we'd come to consider it hers.

Benzer and Franklin sat at the table looking rumpled in their wrinkled T-shirts. In fact, everybody looked a little rumpled, except Bertie of course, who was dressed in tight black pants and a black T-shirt with DIVA written across her chest in rhinestones.

Bertie and Daddy were doing most of the serving. They'd planted Mama in a chair and forbidden her to move a muscle.

"Mama, what's got you so quiet?" Patty asked Aunt Sophie, who was usually running in high gear before most of the adults had swallowed their first sip of coffee.

"I'm worn slap out," she snapped. "Didn't y'all hear that baby crying last night? I swear, it took two hours to get him back to sleep."

Bertie put a handful of cheese into a pot of grits. "Boy, I'd forgotten how grumpy you are in the morning, Sophie," she said.

"You'd be grumpy too, with three hours of sleep."

"Mother, Sophie," Mama said, holding her hands over her ears, "if you wake up the baby, I'll show you grumpy."

"Can I have some ketchup?" Benzer asked.

I passed it over, then pulled my notebook out of the robe's pocket. "Mama, have you guys decided what you're naming the baby?"

"Still not Peyton, but we've been thinking," Daddy answered, sitting down. "Your mama had a good suggestion."

"We thought perhaps it was time to bring the name Walter out of retirement," she said, smiling at me. "What do you think about that? Our very own Louise and Walter."

"Ooooh," Patty said, "maybe y'all can get married."

Franklin rolled his eyes at Patty. "You are such a twelve-year-old."

"I think that's a great idea," I said. I drew a line next to my name on the genealogy chart and wrote in my brother's name. "Walter was a pretty good guy, I guess. He was sort of a hero after all. At least Louise seemed to think so." I frowned. "But it just seems weird that we won't be living here, especially being named after them."

"Well, I think what you're doing is awesome," Benzer said. "My family would have never given that kind of money away."

"Of course not," Bertie said, plopping into a chair. "Yankees have no sense of history."

"Bertie!" I said. "Remember we were going to stop with all the name-calling?"

"Oh, dear, excuse me." She gave me a knowing look.

"I'm sorry, Benzer. I'll try and limit my prejudice against Yank— er, Northerners to the homely ones. Will that work?"

"That depends," he answered. "Have you ever met a Yankee you didn't think was homely?"

"Just one, but you give me hope for the whole lot of them." Bertie winked. "I declare, you two, with all the bad habits I have, you choose this one to break?"

The back door opened, and Isaac came in. "Morning." He placed a casserole dish on the counter. "From my mom."

"Isaac!" I yelled. "Did you hear?"

He turned to me and smiled. "I did. Your dad called me this morning. That's what I wanted to talk to you about."

"Won't Coach Peeler freak when he sees you playing for UT?"

Bertie lifted her coffee mug in a toast gesture, drawing everyone's attention. "Congratulations, Isaac. And speaking of Coach Peeler, guess what I heard while I was at the motel this morning?"

"What?" I asked.

"Doris said the school board was calling an emergency meeting after Lou's interview got everyone talking. People are sick of the superintendent letting Coach Peeler slide."

"It's about time," Daddy said.

"I'll bet twenty dollars he's announced his retirement by Friday," Bertie said.

Patty held up her hand to give me a high five. "I still have to see your interview. I heard your hair looks insane."

As everyone laughed around us, Benzer leaned closer. "I'm sorry you're going to have to move," he whispered. "But we'll still hang out every weekend."

I nodded. "I won't be the girl with the oldest house anymore, but I'll still be a Mayhew. I guess that's good enough."

Benzer rolled his eyes. "Duh! I could have told you that a long time ago."

"Lou," Isaac said, "about the money—"

The doorbell pealed the chorus of "Rocky Top" throughout the house.

"*Rocky Top*," Bertie started, and we all joined in, "*you'll always be, home, sweet home, to me!*"

"Don't wake the baby," Mama said, going to the door.

"Walter," I called after her, "his name is Walter."

"Tucker, I hope you can take that doorbell with you," Bertie said.

The door swung open, and Mama walked back into the kitchen. On her heels was George Neely.

From the diary of Louise Duncan Mayhew
April 1864

We received news that the Yanks were camped a few miles away. Olivia hid the most important things behind the bookshelf, while Molly and I rolled a barrel with our food stores into the woods. We could barely finish for staring over our shoulders like frightened deer. Before long, a group of about 20 rode into the yard, firing their muskets, and walking through the house as though they owned it. We were fortunate that they found little to interest them other than our last silver cup and our candle wax.

———

Benzer, Franklin, and I stared at him. I couldn't have been more surprised if Mama had walked inside with an alien on her arm.

Mama offered her hand to Mr. Neely. "Good morning. I don't believe we've met."

"George Neely, historian. How do you do?" He nodded at everyone. "I believe I met these young folks recently, at the museum and . . ." His voice trailed off when he got to Patty, as if he was trying to place her.

Patty had sunk so low into her chair that she was in danger of falling onto the floor.

"I'm sorry to barge in on you this morning, but I was just having breakfast at the motel and heard the most extraordinary thing."

"Mother!" Aunt Sophie said. "You couldn't even make it one day."

Bertie raised her eyebrows. "No one told me not to say anything."

"It was more of an unspoken rule, Mother."

"Well, that's the craziest thing I've ever heard," Bertie said with a sniff. "You can't break an 'unspoken rule.' That's why they're spoken."

"So it's true?" Mr. Neely said, coming to hover over my chair. "You really did find it?"

I pushed my plate away. "I knew it! I told the rest of them that you were looking for it too. Well, you can forget about it. It's already been given away. Every last piece."

"What?" Mr. Neely looked like he was going to keel over.

Isaac motioned him to take a chair. "You look like you need to sit."

Mr. Neely sank onto the ladder-back chair. He really did look ill. "I don't understand. Was it in such poor shape? Who did you give it to? I could help. I know people who specialize in that type of conservation."

Bertie sipped her coffee. "Are you crazy? The gold is in fine shape. All thirty-seven pieces look like they were minted this morning."

He gasped loudly. "That many pieces? Oh, my goodness, I've got to call the museum. They are never going to believe this. But that's not what I am talking about—please, tell me about the diary."

I stared at him, puzzled. "Wait. Weren't you looking for the gold?"

"Oh, heavens no. I would have never believed it was still around, not after all these years. I would have thought it had been spent ages ago." He looked around the table at our confused faces. "No, I've been searching for the diary." He pulled a worn piece of paper out of his shirt pocket and held it up for us to see. "This is a copy of a letter written by Miss Olivia McDonald to her colleagues at Vanderbilt in the year 1884. In it she mentions quite clearly a diary kept by her cousin, Louise Duncan Mayhew. I did my doctorate on Olivia McDonald, you know. Quite the forward thinker for her time."

I leaned back in my chair and pulled the diary off the buffet. "Do you mean this diary?"

Mr. Neely let out a high-pitched squeal. "Can I see it?" he asked breathlessly.

Without a word, I handed it over.

"Is he gonna cry?" Benzer whispered.

"Shhh," Mama said, kicking him under the table.

It wouldn't have mattered what we said, since he wasn't listening. He was staring at the diary like he'd found his long-lost love. He turned the pages carefully. "Oh, just look at this. It's in wonderful shape." Looking at me across the table, he asked, "Where did you find it?"

"It was in the old chest we got at the Tate Brothers auction."

"My goodness, right under my nose," he said, stroking the pages. "After all this time, here it is."

"If you wanted to know about our family, why didn't you just ask?" Mama said.

"I did make inquiries the night of the museum opening," Mr. Neely said. He looked at Daddy. "But I was told your family didn't want the past revisited."

"Oh," Dad said, grinning sheepishly. "I guess in hindsight that wasn't so smart."

"Dad!" I reminded him. "Didn't your grandfather say it was important to remember our history?"

"You're right, Lou. You should never be afraid of the

past. It's how we learn." He shook his head. "I should have known better."

I smiled. "It would be nice to learn things every now and then without having to hide in a closet!"

Mama nodded. "I agree. Lou is old enough to be told the truth, even when it's not particularly pleasant."

Bertie stood and held out a plate to Mr. Neely. "You might as well eat something while you're here."

"Oh, I couldn't eat a thing," he replied. "I'm much too excited. Have you read it? Did it mention anything about the Underground Railroad?"

Bertie dropped the plate with a thud. "The Underground Railroad?"

Mr. Neely nodded. "We know that Olivia McDonald was heavily involved in helping slaves, and since she stayed here for a time, we were hoping to prove she used this house as a station."

I shook my head. "It mentions her trying to help slaves, but I didn't see anything about using the house."

"That's unfortunate. Not surprising, as most people were too careful to write about it, but still one can dream," Mr. Neely said.

"May I see Olivia's letter?" Bertie asked. "I'd love to have a copy for our museum."

"Of course." Mr. Neely handed the worn piece of paper across the table, and Bertie picked it up, reading silently.

Patty had recovered enough that I could almost see her whole head. She pointed to a picture on the back of the letter. "What's that?"

"Oh, those are some of my research notes. That is the mark of Samuel Bunting," Mr. Neely said. "One of the slaves Olivia helped escape."

"Why would he need a 'mark'?" Benzer asked.

Mr. Neely smiled as Mama handed him a biscuit. He said, "Slaves weren't taught to read or write, and that mark is how he signed his name. After he was freed, he became a renowned silversmith, and the bunting is how he marked his pieces. Some of his earlier ones are quite valuable."

I leaned in closer to look. "I've seen that mark."

Everyone turned to stare at me.

"You've seen that particular mark, Lou?" Daddy asked. "Where?"

"In a couple of places, I think. C'mon, I'll show you." I pushed my chair away from the table and stood. Everyone stood with me and followed me down the hallway. I led them into the parlor, where my slave chest was.

Mr. Neely gasped. "So here's the famous slave chest!"

I pointed to the carving. "Isn't that the same bird?"

"My word. Look at the detail!" Mr. Neely exclaimed. "If this is a real Bunting, it has to be one of the oldest pieces I've seen."

"I thought he was a silversmith," Isaac said.

"Yes, later. But he was a talented furniture maker as well."

Mama ran a hand across the top of the chest. "I can hardly believe it. You said you'd seen it a couple of places, Lou. Where else?"

"Here." I moved to the bookcase and tugged on the corner to reveal the room behind.

"Has that room always been there?" Aunt Sophie asked, wide-eyed.

Daddy laughed. "It's why we can't keep secrets in this family. We figure it's where the family hid valuables during the Civil War."

I turned on the light and pointed to the corner. "It's over near the floor."

Mr. Neely moved forward and knelt as everyone crowded around him, blocking out most of the light. "I'd have to take an impression and have it authenticated, but it looks like his mark to me!"

The room was just as hot as ever, so as soon as Mr. Neely had finished looking around, we moved back into the parlor.

"So if this Bunting fellow was here, scratching birds in our hidden room, surely that points to this house being used on the Underground Railroad," Bertie said. "Right?"

Mr. Neely took a handkerchief out of his pocket and wiped his brow. "It takes a lot to prove these things, but if the bunting can be authenticated, I believe in time we'll be able to say yes with a great deal of confidence."

"Time is the one thing we don't have," I said, frowning. "The county is planning on tearing down the house."

"Tear down this house? I don't understand," Mr. Neely said.

"Yeah, me neither," I said dejectedly. "But they're stealing it through eminent domain."

Mr. Neely shook his head. "Oh, no, this won't do. Destroy a house of such historical significance? Never!"

Franklin cleared his throat. "I've been hoping to get Lou's house onto the National Register of Historic Places. Perhaps that would be easier now, in light of the recent discoveries."

"I should say so. I am an official Tennessee review board member for the National Register. If this house doesn't qualify, I don't know what would!"

"Would that really be enough to stop them?" Mama asked.

"My good lady," Mr. Neely said, "I'd camp on the governor's lawn before I'd let them tear down this house!"

"Wow, Mr. Neely," I said, "you're the best! This means I get to stay!"

"And I'm going to get my badge!" Franklin crowed.

"And Isaac is going to play for Tennessee!" I said.

"Best summer ever!" Benzer said. "And Pete Winningham can stick it—you won, Lou!"

"Lou," Isaac said, "that's what I've been trying to talk to you about. I can't take all that money!"

Everyone got quiet, and I stared at Isaac in disbelief. "What are you saying? You have to. It's the plan!"

He smiled. "What I mean is, I'd like to just use part of the money."

"Part?" Daddy asked. "But how will you pay for school?"

"I figure with some of the money, and by working at the university, I can afford tuition for one year without too much trouble."

"But what about the next year?" I asked.

He shrugged. "I'm giving myself one season to show Coach Fuller what I can do. If I can't get a scholarship after that, I'll transfer."

"Oh, you will definitely get a scholarship, but the money is yours. I'm happy to give it all to you." I grinned. "Especially now that the house is saved."

"Well, what do you think about donating the rest of the money to the new minority scholarship fund? I'm not the only person in town that could use help. The town's actually raised a lot of money, and with this, it will go a long way in helping other kids get to college."

"That would be awesome!" I said.

"Whoo, if that don't get your fire started, your wood is wet," Bertie said. She smiled at Isaac for a moment, then came to give me a hug. "Child, what kind of prayer was that, anyway?"

I hugged Bertie, then Sophie, Daddy and Mama, Isaac, and even Mr. Neely.

"I'd better get back home," Isaac said. "My mom's calling everyone she knows to tell them I'm playing in the SEC. I keep telling her I'm just a walk-on, but she's convinced I'm their new star player."

"It's only a matter of time," Daddy said.

The grown-ups asked us to clean away the breakfast dishes while they got more coffee and went into the den to make plans.

Benzer punched my arm lightly. "You must be feeling great—Isaac's going to UT, and you saved your house."

"Me?" I asked. "Don't you mean we?"

"Yeah," Patty said, helping herself to a leftover biscuit. "I believe I helped. Without me, you'd still be stuck under George Neely's bed."

"I agree," Franklin said. "It was an excellent team effort."

"We did it," Benzer corrected himself. "And now we'll still have this house to hang out in. Cool!"

I looked around the kitchen. The counter had a small scar from where I'd tripped once and hit the corner with my tooth, and a portion of the wallpaper was peeling. It was where my high chair used to sit, and Mama said I'd skinned half the wall before they got me eating solid foods. Bertie's mugs, all with funny sayings, hung on hooks behind the sink. It was the most beautiful kitchen I'd ever seen.

"Hey," said Franklin, piling a stack of plates into the sink, "let's go outside where the stump used to be. Come on, Lou. Maybe you missed some gold."

"I'll meet you out there," I said. "I've got something to do first."

They laughed and ran out the door. I stopped at the entry to the den and listened as George Neely read from the diary, the words of Louise Mayhew drifting through the air. Bertie interrupted him to ask a question, and Aunt Sophie snored softly in a chair. I saw Mama and Daddy leaning against each other on the couch, seeming happy just to watch everyone.

I walked quietly past, into the parlor. The morning light reflected off the gold lettering of the Bible's spine as I pulled it from the shelf. Kneeling, I opened it to the front page where Silas Whittle's name was still legible.

"God," I whispered, "thank you for saving my house, for giving me a new brother, and for letting Isaac go to UT." Wow, this had been some summer, after all. I sat, thinking. "I'm sorry I thought you were a fuddy-duddy, and don't take this the wrong way, but if my brother ever says a stupid prayer, could you just let it slide? Amen."

I turned to the back and pulled out Walter's letter to

Louise, then placed the Bible as high on the shelf as I could reach.

"I thought I saw you come in here." Bertie leaned against the door frame. "Don't hide that Bible. I may need it sometime."

"No way! I'm putting this Bible away. I don't think you can be trusted."

"You could be right." She smiled. "And have you had enough excitement for a while?"

"Totally, although I can see now why you love history so much. It's actually kinda awesome."

"Now that you like it too, you can be the official family historian."

I stared at her. "Is that a real thing?"

"If it's not, it ought to be. Somebody's got to make sure we don't forget what's important."

I nodded. "That's the only reason I can stand looking at slave quarters in the backyard. It's our job to remember."

"That's my girl. You want to volunteer sometime at the museum with me? We could take turns driving Thelma Johnson crazy."

"Sure," I said. "It was fun learning about Walter and Louise. Daddy's family was pretty cool."

"Oh, that's nothing. You should hear some of the stories about *my* side of the family."

I laughed. "I can't wait!" I handed her the letter. "This

was in the Bible. I thought you might like it for the museum."

She read it carefully. "This is remarkable. And it was in our Bible the whole time?"

"Yep. Maybe somebody should have opened it a little more often!"

Benzer yelled in to me from the front door. "Lou, are you coming? Franklin got word that Sally Martin and her friends are at the Piggly Wiggly. If we hurry, we can catch them. I can't wait until you tell her about your summer. She might be shocked speechless for once!"

"I'll be right there," I shouted back. "Bertie, it's so amazing to think this house was part of the Underground Railroad. Louise and Olivia must have been seriously brave."

"Yes," Bertie answered. "They ultimately rebelled against their own neighbors *and* the Confederate government. That took a lot of gumption." She put a hand on my cheek. "You know, that sounds a lot like you."

"I only rebelled against Pete Winningham."

"And Coach Peeler," Bertie said. "Girl, you come from a long line of rebels. If these walls could talk, you'd be one of their stories!" Bertie gave me a hug. "I'm proud of you, child! You've got more backbone than a peacock's got tail."

"Thanks, Bertie. But in case you haven't heard, Mayhews are made of steel!"

She laughed. "They sure are. But I'm not a Mayhew, remember. My people are made of spunk, and it looks like you got your fair share of that too. We may be more alike than you think."

I looked at where Benzer had been standing moments ago. "You know, I'm beginning to think that's not such a bad thing," I said, smiling. And with a wink, I raced outside.

From the diary of Louise Duncan Mayhew
July 1865

I can scarce believe the War has ended. I am much changed from the girl I was when this conflict started, as is this Country, but I'd have neither of us return. So many things I held to be true have been proven false. The desolation is all around us, in the ruined homes and broken families, yet I do not fall into despair for there is also hope. I see it in the lavender violet just beginning to bloom in the meadow, and on the faces of my resilient neighbors.

Yesterday, Mr. Harris delivered a crate addressed to Olivia and me. There was no name attached, but upon opening I knew immediately that it was from Samuel. Inside was a wood chest adorned with beautifully carved buntings. It contained a single piece of paper with drawn instructions on how to open a secret compartment. On the back, a drawing of a tree with three birds perched and singing from its branches. Olivia said I must keep it, as a "tangible symbol of my redemption and efforts toward the cause." Yes, there is hope for us all yet.

Speaking of secrets, Diary, I do have one more to impart. I have not seen the doctor, but I know, a woman knows. We are going to have a baby! I will tell Walter tonight. Imagine, a baby of our own, to carry on the Mayhew name. God is so good.

ACKNOWLEDGMENTS

T his book would be nothing but a dream of mine without the wonderful encouragement and guidance of so many. I am eternally grateful to Deborah Osgood and Steve Bock, who have cheered for Lou from the beginning; to Cay Drew and her sons, who gave Lou her first middle-grade stamp of approval; to Coach Matthan Houser (who is everything Coach Peeler is not) for sharing his vast football knowledge; and to Pastor David Eldridge for encouraging me to do my "deal."

Thank you to the Society of Children's Book Writers and Illustrators for their kind support and the Middle Grade Mafia for their friendship. The feedback from friends and fellow writers Debbie D'Aurelio, Alison Hertz, Kim Zachman, Kevin Springer, L. S. Bridgers, and Kristine Anderson was invaluable.

I am profoundly thankful to my agent, Susan Hawk. I've heard there is no such thing as a perfect agent, but, Susan, you are proof that there is! To my incredible editor, Nancy Paulsen, you have been a beautiful blessing on my life. Every round of edits made this book better, and it has been an honor to work with you. Thank you to Sara LaFleur and the entire team at Nancy Paulsen Books for your hard work behind the scenes to make this the best possible version of *Rebels*. Gilbert Ford, you are an artistic genius.

To Tania Stephens, Ellery Lewis, and the rest of my crazy family, your sense of humor has heavily influenced my life and this book. To my friends in Hog-Eye Country, your presence is in every line.

Thank you, JD and Rachel, for your unwavering belief that this day would come. I can't imagine life without you by my side.

And finally, I pray every word of *Rebels* gives truth to Colossians 3:17.

Lou's search through her history was painful, but in the end there was redemption. I'm thankful that no matter what our own pasts contain, there is hope for the same.

Thank you for reading.